A Rachel Markham Mystery

MURDER

AT RAVENROCK

BOOK 2 - IN THE MYSTERY SERIES

D1560000

A Rachel Markham Mystery

MURDER

AT RAVENROCK

BOOK 2 - IN THE MYSTERY SERIES

P.B. KOLLERI

notionpress.com

Notion Press

First published by NotionPress 2013

Copyright © P.B Kolleri 2013

All Rights Reserved.

ISBN: 978-14-82721-63-8

This book is a labour of love dedicated to
Aanya – my daughter, my friend.

'The sins of the father are to be laid upon the children.'
Shakespeare
The Merchant of Venice (3.5.1)

Chapter One

DARTMOUTH. MAY 1947.

'Good morning, my darling. Would you like some tea?' Jeremy asked his wife, Rachel, as she stretched luxuriously under the covers and opened her eyes. He was standing by the window, dressed casually for the day, reading the morning paper. A good looking man, Jeremy had an aquiline nose, and deep set brown eyes that shone with good natured affection, as he looked at his wife. She sat up in bed and gave him a sleepy smile.

'In a while. Did you catch any worms yet, my early riser?' Rachel grinned at him, her auburn curls framing her beautiful face. Rachel had just turned twenty four, a week ago, and there was a youthful glow about her, along with a dazzling smile that always reached her expressive green eyes.

'No such luck, my beautiful, unless of course you categorize Inspector Parker as one,' he smiled back. It always amazed him that she got up looking so dewy fresh every morning. *How did I get so lucky*, he thought to himself.

'I don't think he'll be very pleased, if I did,' Rachel said, grinning as she got out of bed, and wrapped her red silk kimono dressing gown, over her exquisite French ivory lace peignoir. Both had been wedding gifts from her close friend and aunt by relation - Celia.

'I suppose not. As much as I'd like to stay, and chat with my beautiful wife, I must join the Inspector at the cafe. There is some fresh tea here but I'm afraid you've missed your worms this morning. They've finished serving breakfast downstairs. We could get you something to eat at the cafe. Thought you may want to pick and choose according to your mood this morning, my love,' Jeremy said as he came forward to give her a morning kiss.

'No thank you, darling,' she said as she gave him a kiss, and continued in a mock grief stricken voice, 'tsk, tsk... feeling sorry for myself...married six months and deserted already... for the devastating charms of Inspector Parker.'

'Now *that* I'm sure, he'll be very happy to hear,' Jeremy said sardonically.

'Yes dear, do go and make his day. I think, I'll just grab a Cornish pasty downstairs; despite food rations, they seem to be overflowing with those things here. Quite nice too. Post which, my plan is - to go down to that secret sandy cove for a swim and drown my sorrows,' she said, referring to a small cove they had discovered on the coastal path, across the river, where they had gone walking the day before.

'Right, do be careful darling. It did have a sign that said 'Private' you know,' Jeremy warned her.

'Oh, don't be such an old woman, Jeremy! Even if someone does catch me swimming there, what will they do, prosecute me? I'll just pretend I'm a beautiful brainless tourist, who can't read signs and worm my way out of it, don't you worry, dear.' She grinned.

'It's precisely this sort of reckless behaviour that gives me sleepless nights about you, dear.' Jeremy told her.

'What sleepless nights? I'll have you know, Jeremy Richards, that you snore like a steam train chugging away cheerfully, on most nights.' She retorted cheekily.

'Really?' He asked her, with his characteristic amused look, with one raised eyebrow.

'Alright, darling, perhaps I am exaggerating a wee bit, but do stop fussing so much. I'll be fine,' she said, smiling at him brightly.

'Fine but don't be too long, dear or I'll have to do a lot of extra hard work, to come looking for you, all the way across the river,' Jeremy said.

Rachel rolled her eyes and replied. 'Stop worrying! I'll meet you back at the cafe after an hour or two, and give you the pleasure of feeding me an enormous lunch.'

'Right then, I'll be off now, for my tryst with your charming Inspector. Try not to fall off the ferry, or get arrested, until lunchtime, darling,' Jeremy said, teasing her, and dodging a small cushion that came flying at him.

After Jeremy left the room, Rachel smiled to herself, *it's lovely to be happily married.* She walked to the bay window, overlooking the harbour on beautiful River Dart. It was a sunlit May morning, and the river reflected a thousand slivers of silver light. She looked up to see a few white cotton clouds, floating across a white and blue sky. One of the clouds reminded her of a ship floating across in full sail. Another, resembled an animal, a large hound or a horse. As it drifted by, changing shape, the Sun peeked out from behind it, and shone brilliantly into her eyes. She lowered her eyes to the hills across the river. She could see the white house on the hill, on the other side of the quay, shaded by the clouds. As the clouds moved, its window panes began reflecting sunlight, and it seemed to come alive. From a distance, it looked, like it was made of sparkling snow, on an emerald hill. *There is so much beauty all around,* she thought to herself. Satisfied with her life in general, she took off the striped navy blue and white tea cosy, and poured herself a comforting cup of fragrant tea. As the aroma of tea wafted through the air, she sat on the cushions in the alcove of the bay window.

The seat at the bay window reminded her of her room at her Uncle Charles' home - 'Rutherford Hall'. So much had happened there. In her mind's eye, time stood still, as if it had all happened yesterday. She recollected the momentous events, which had taken place six months ago, and changed the destiny of all involved. The fateful day, she had met her future husband for the first time. The same day, her Uncle Charles had been brutally murdered. His beautiful young wife, Celia, had been one of the many suspects in the investigation. Up until

Rachel and Jeremy had decided to team up and unravel the mystery surrounding his murder.

She sighed, as she thought of Uncle Charles. He had been so kind to her, to them all. A gentle being, who had been mercilessly killed simply for being at the wrong place, at the wrong time. Life is strange that way, you never know what's in store, Rachel mused. Anyhow, one could take some solace in the fact that they had the final satisfaction of catching the real killer and saving yet another innocent from dying at the gallows. It could have been worse. All evidence had pointed otherwise, and had it not been for Rachel and Jeremy, in all likelihood, a jury would have hung the wrong person based on the case files and police evidence.

Their stay so far at Dartmouth, ostensibly on a holiday, was a cover up for trying to get to the bottom of yet another baffling case. Rachel had bullied Jeremy into getting involved and the Inspector had welcomed their presence. He knew, if the last case was anything to go by, he could use their help in solving this one. The Inspector had been invited, by the Superintendent of Police to 'look into the case' at Devon, since he had done 'so well' at cracking the case, at Rutherford Hall. But, he also knew that the local investigating officer, Inspector Thomas would not be too pleased having to play second fiddle to Parker.

Placed in the uncomfortable situation of being in another man's territory, it gave him some degree of confidence, to have *the* Jeremy Richards by his side. Besides, Jeremy's erstwhile luminous career, as a detective at Scotland Yard, had a formidable way of opening otherwise closed doors in police circles. Jeremy had taken early retirement from the Yard, to get away from it all. He had moved to the country, to supposedly lead a peaceful life, only to find himself embroiled neck-deep in the murder case at Rutherford Hall. And now, thanks to her insistence, along with subtle hints, and positive nudges from the Inspector, he found himself in Dartmouth on yet another case. It had been three days, since they had arrived at Dartmouth, and so far they had very little to go on. Rachel thought to herself, about Jeremy's predicament, and smiled. *Ah well, everyone knows, that which you try to run from, in life, invariably follows you, no matter where you go, until you make your peace with it.* Somewhere, she knew instinctively, that Jeremy was yet to be at peace with his sudden decision, to quit his role at Scotland Yard. After a particularly brutal case, where he felt he had failed, as a human being. He had succeeded, as an officer of the law, in tracking down the killer but had failed to reach in time, to save a child from a vicious murderer.

The shrill sound of the telephone ringing brought her back to the present. She put her cup down, and walked over to the bedside table, to lift the receiver.

A man's voice said, 'Hello, Miss Rachel. This is Inspector Parker. Might I speak with your husband?'

Rachel smiled at the Inspector's usage of 'Miss' out of habit. Her being a 'Mrs.' was taking a lot of getting used to, especially for those who had known her since she was a girl. Out loud she said, 'Good morning, Inspector. Jeremy just left. You'll probably run into him at the cafe. That is where he's headed.'

The Inspector said, 'That's just it. I called to inform him that I can't make it to the cafe. There have been certain developments in the case, and I've just been informed that another body washed up yesterday, by the cove near Mill Bay...er...I'd rather not go into all that, just yet. If you could just leave a message for him, to come by to the Police Station...'

'I can do better than that, Inspector. I could find him and bring him over to the Station. Give me fifteen minutes.' She hung up before he could respond, and rushed to get dressed. *I'll catch Jeremy at the cafe, if I'm quick, and then find out what these developments, in the case, are all about. So long, Cornish pasty and lazy morning swim,* she thought to herself.

Chapter Two

On the other side of the river, on the terrace of the white house that Rachel had been admiring from her bay window earlier, Helen Cavendish stood on the edge of the railing, peering below. The house had been renamed Falcon's Crest by its latest owner – her father, the fifty four year old, whimsical millionaire Henry Cavendish, whose passionate pursuits included taking bird watching safaris around the world, when he got tired of romancing beautiful women, or raking in more money than he could spend, through his diverse business interests across the globe. His only daughter – Helen, heiress to his fortune, was looking down upon River Dart, searching for a certain white yacht, with intertwined blue and silver stripes on its sides. A tall willowy girl in her mid twenties, she had straight blond, shoulder length hair, and Nordic features, high cheek bones and striking blue-green eyes. Despite her near perfect features, something in the way they all came together, gave her face character, but stopped short of being, what one would normally describe, as classically beautiful.

She was loose limbed, and it was easy to tell, that she must have been rather gawky, as a teenager. At twenty four, she still looked very young for her age, and had always felt awkward about her appearance. That very morning, she had been critically judging her appearance in the mirror. She felt that her nose was too long and her eyes were too small. Her only redeeming feature, to her mind, was that she had beautiful hands with long tapering fingers. The hands of an artist – as her father always told her, with distinct pride. To that end, after attending finishing school, she had dabbled in art and painting for a while, without much success. She had come to the practical self-realization, early in life, unlike most ego-centric artists, that at best, her art could only be termed as mediocre. There was something missing from her art – it lacked that edge to take it to the next level, which made all the difference. Of late, she had taken on sculpting, to see if that was the right niche for her artistic expression. Her father had indulged her by creating a sculpting studio of sorts, within the existing garden shed. The rustic, wooden sculpting table was in the center of the shed, surrounded by odds and ends along with a few gardening tools, required to maintain the extensive grounds of Falcon's Crest.

She had moved back to England, from Switzerland, a year ago, and accepted the invitation to live at Dartmouth, with her father and her new stepmother – the beautiful American actress Sofia Burnett. So far, she had found her stepmother to be a fun loving, interesting and enigmatic person but of late, she was beginning to sense a discord between the couple. Nothing she could quite put her finger on, as there was no visible change in either her father's or Sofia's behaviour towards her, but there was a certain atmosphere of strain in the household. She was an artist at heart, and she was sensitive to vibrations – especially the unhappy kind. And now, for the first time since they had gotten married, her father had left Sofia behind at Dartmouth, to spend two weeks at his club in London. Sofia, on the other hand, seemed to be completely unruffled by his departure and in higher spirits than usual. Perhaps, that was just a front to hide her true feelings. Something was definitely wrong and the strain was getting on her nerves. Helen wanted a change of scene, desperately. When her neighbour, Timothy Wilson had called earlier in the week and proposed a weekend trip on his yacht, she readily agreed. To that end, she eagerly awaited his arrival in the harbour below. Her overnight bag was packed and kept on the terrace.

'Oh, Helen honey, have you seen this?' Sofia came out on to the deck waving a newspaper about, in her usual dramatic style. She was dressed in a stark white pantsuit, with a stylish white cape thrown over it – cut in the latest fashion that caused quite a sensation, even in the most fashionable circles in America. The war had brought about a change in dress allowances and what started out as a practical venture, undertaken by working women, to beat clothing rations by wearing their husband's trousers, had now become a rage in high society. Especially among very wealthy women, who had never really experienced anything close to hard manual labour, which had started the trend, in the first place. Trousers were gradually becoming a fashion statement for the free thinking woman, and young women in England too had started taking a shine to wearing trousers, although it still shocked conservative sensibilities. It was just like Sofia to have a wardrobe full of them, in all colours. She liked to create a sensation wherever she went.

Helen smiled at Sofia and answered her query, 'No. I haven't read the paper today. Was busy packing for my yachting trip. What is it?'

'It's that fellow from the quayside tearoom, the other day. The day we had gone to town with John. You remember the awful man that came up to the table to get my autograph?' She said, referring to their recent outing with their friend and neighbour Captain John Griffin - He was a thirty year old widower who had fought in the war. He lived close by at Ravenrock House. Sofia thought him a tad dull, but still entertained him a great deal. She found him rather attractive in a strange way. He was not much of a conversationalist but his lean face, beaked nose and piercing grey eyes gave him a certain aura. To her mind he was a figure out of a tragedy – a lost soul who had tragically lost his wife and child, while he was away fighting the war. From her point of view, she was just doing her bit to spread sweetness and light in the world. Besides, she was convinced that the company of a woman, especially one as beautiful as her always had a cheering effect on most men and the good captain was no exception.

'Ah yes, I remember the man. He was a tad scruffy. The one, John threw out. God only knows, how they let him in. These places are really going to the dogs these days. But, what about him? He hasn't been bothering you, has he?' Helen asked, in a concerned voice.

'It would be quite a feat if he could, honey. It says here, he went and drowned himself. His body washed up at Mill Bay, yesterday. Some tourists found him. There's a picture of him in this,' she said, holding out the newspaper.

'How awful! Yes, I do recognize him, even though he looks a lot better in this picture,' Helen said taking a closer look at the old army picture, possibly taken from the drowned man's belongings.

'Must be the uniform. Ex-army, they say.'

'Yes, don't you remember - he recognized John as his commanding officer?'

Sofia responded by scrunching up her nose, 'All I remember is that he had this awful beer breath and I almost gagged!'

'He called John by a funny army nickname – 'Dusty,' I think it was...' Helen remembered.

'I can't imagine immaculate Captain John Griffin being known as Dusty by his soldiers! What these boys must have gone through in the war. It's hard to imagine,' Sofia said, with a faraway look.

'And he made some rude comments about us to John - something on the lines of, 'you've done well for yourself Dusty John! A pretty lass on each arm!' Helen mimicked the drunken man.

'I don't think that was the least bit rude. The leering

way he said it, probably was. Once you get to my age, being referred to as a 'pretty lass', is quite the compliment,' Sofia said, facetiously.

'You are only forty, Sofia!' Helen laughed out.

'Hush child. I'll never admit to a day over thirty in public!' Sofia retorted.

'That is funny, but nonetheless, he definitely managed to get John's back up,' Helen said.

'Oh yes! It was rather amusing. I've never seen dull John so worked up. It was magnificent. The way he stood up and simply roared at the man, 'That's Captain John Griffin to you – you disreputable bugger!" Sofia said, making full use of her indisputable talent as an actress.

'I thought the funniest bit was when the 'disreputable bugger' said 'Aye, aye, Cap'n, gave John a wink and keeled right over as he clicked his heels in his attempted salute!' Helen said, mimicking the salute.

'He must've been quite drunk. He nearly fell on you! If John hadn't broken his fall he could have done you an injury,' Sofia said, thinking back to the scene the man had caused in the tearoom.

'But John didn't have to throw him out by the scruff of his neck. I thought that was a bit extreme, didn't you?' Helen ventured.

'My dear! I thought that was rather gallant, don't you think? Made me see John in an entirely new light. Never knew he was such a caveman. Suddenly, I want to get to know him better,' Sofia said, coquettishly fluttering her eyelids.

'Really, Sofia! If I didn't know you better, that statement would've had me worried. Sometimes I think you enjoy scandalizing people, just for the sake of it,' Helen admonished her.

'Just sometimes, honey? I do it all the time. Spices things up a bit, in life,' Sofia chuckled.

'Be careful, darling. Someday, someone may take the spiced up things you say seriously and the consequences may not be so rum,' she said, in a warning note.

'Oh honey, you're much too young to be so serious. This world is already full of dull, serious types. You really need to lighten up and look, there's someone's jumping up and down on that boat, waving at us,' Sofia said, pointing at the yacht on River Dart.

'Oh goody, that's Timothy. He's arrived! I'll be running along then. You take care of yourself, darling and be good to Dad, once he gets back,' Helen said, picking up her overnight bag from the table on the terrace, and blowing a kiss in her stepmother's direction.

'I'm always good. Have fun, honey and don't do anything I wouldn't do!' Sofia told her stepdaughter.

'Right! That gives me a licence to do just about anything then,' Helen chuckled, as she ran down the steps, leading to the boathouse below.

Chapter Three

Jeremy and Rachel had reached the police station in twenty minutes. Located on Mayor's Avenue, on a cobblestoned street, it was one of the prettiest locations for a police station, Rachel had ever seen. She had commented on that to Jeremy, the first time they had been there.

Now, as they walked in, they were greeted by Constable Goole, seated behind the big oak desk, and he told them that Inspector Parker was in Inspector Thomas' room, and they could go right in. They had been introduced to Inspector Thomas and his team on their arrival at Dartmouth, three days ago.

As Jeremy knocked, before he popped his head in through the door to announce their arrival, he heard Inspector Thomas' voice boom, 'It's about time! We could use some more cooks around here – to cook our goose right and proper! Come on in, Detective Richards. This is the third death, related to that cursed Ravenrock place. They seem to be dropping like flies. Just don't understand why, anyone who goes near that place winds up dead! The pressure has started mounting. We've got to get to the bottom of this, and fast.' He slammed his fist down on the table, in sheer frustration. Inspector Thomas was a big built man with red cheeks, a bushy moustache and a hearty manner. Rachel thought that, given a good costume, he would make the perfect Santa to entertain children, around Christmas. Although, at the moment he looked like a very cross Santa – one that was suffering from a touch of dyspepsia, perhaps.

His appearance was in complete contrast to Inspector Parker, who had always reminded Rachel of a friendly village grocer. Inspector Parker, who had been watching the scene placidly, got up to greet Jeremy in his own quiet way and offered Rachel a chair.

She thanked him and asked Inspector Parker, 'So, this death is related to Ravenrock House too?'

Inspector Parker addressed her, 'In a way it is. This time, we are actually a little more clueless. The man - Mike Murray was a vagabond. Captain John Griffin informed us that he recognised him, as a deserter from one of his platoons. The man's personal effects were found stashed behind a rock, at the cove, where his body was found. He had a small holdall that contained some clothes, and a wallet with some Italian currency, mixed with a few shillings and a piece of paper that had the address and clear directions to Ravenrock House. We have no idea, who he was supposed to meet there, but the Italian currency points to an Italian connection.'

Inspector Thomas cut in at this point, 'We have contacted Judge Wilson to find out the whereabouts of his Italian son-in-law, Antonio Baloney but we were told that he and his wife were off on a cruise, somewhere upriver, with young Timothy Wilson and their neighbour Miss Cavendish. They left this morning. We've wired all the stations around, to keep an eye out for 'Charisma' – the yacht in question. The port command is also trying to reach them on wireless, but there seems to be some trouble with the yacht's radio receiver. They haven't got a response yet. But the river police are on the lookout too, and if they dock anywhere on River Dart, they will be informed and brought in for questioning.'

Jeremy spoke up at this point, 'That makes sense. But let's not jump to any conclusions, based on the Italian lire found on the dead man. It could be that like a lot of deserters, he took refuge in Italy, after he deserted and was hired by someone to come here for a purpose. But, we can't be sure about that. Did you find a passport among his things?'

Inspector Thomas shifted uncomfortably and said, 'No, now that you mention it, we didn't. That is strange. He couldn't have re-entered England without one, if he did in fact come in from Italy. We may find out more about the drowned man's Italian connections to the family, once we get the Italian son-in-law in for questioning.'

Rachel spoke up, 'I wasn't aware that Judge Wilson's son-in-law was Italian. He seemed quite English when we met him, the other day.'

Inspector Thomas intervened, 'That must have been the other son-in-law, Captain John Griffin. He's English alright, pukka sahib. Fought in the war.'

'How many son-in-laws does he have?' Rachel asked, confused.

Inspector Thomas smiled and replied by way of explanation, 'at last count – two. Judge Wilson and his late wife Dorothy had four children, three daughters and a son. The eldest child Pamela was married to John Griffin and she died in the Torquay bombing in 1944. The second oldest, his daughter Evelyn, who is very much alive and is married to this Italian race car driver chappy - Antonio Baloney. Followed by the third - a boy, Timothy Wilson who just got back from University a year ago and is rather keen on sailing. And pretty good at it too, from what I hear. He damn near won the Dartmouth Royal Regatta last year. Apart from a sail boat for the regatta, the Judge also bought him this yacht – the one we're looking for at the moment. The fourth child, the youngest – a girl called Adelaide, drowned under mysterious circumstances, three weeks ago. She was only fourteen when she died and from all accounts, she was a bit soft in the head.'

'Abnormal, you mean?' Jeremy asked.

'Yes, you see, her mother Dorothy, died at childbirth and local lore is that the child was born with an abnormally large head, probably caused by excess water in the brain. She was seen to by a host of child specialists on Harley Street, who recommended that the child be institutionalised. But Judge Wilson's sister, Edith wouldn't hear of it and she finally brought up the girl by herself, at her house in Torquay. Under her special care, the child Adelaide did exceptionally well and by the time she was ten, she was almost normal and started attending the local school. But they say the demolition of their house in Torquay, during the bombing and consequently the death of her older sister – Pamela, had a bad affect on her. Both Edith and Adelaide moved to Ravenrock at Dartmouth soon afterwards. She seemed to recover somewhat, with the change of scene, but she was traumatised by the bombing, and I don't suppose, she was ever entirely normal to begin with.'

'You believe she was murdered?' Rachel asked him.

'Yes, for the simple reason that the child was scared to death of water, owing to a childhood incident when she almost drowned. According to the family, she didn't know how to swim and wouldn't have gone anywhere near the river on her own. And yet, when her body washed up, she was in a bathing suit. Looked as though, someone had put her in a bathing suit and thrown her into the river to drown.'

'Ugh, how awful!' Rachel said.

'Yes. It was rather. The sinister thing was that the night before, while the whole family was at dinner, she had said that *she knew who had killed her Aunt Edith -* who had died a week before that, again under mysterious circumstances. The inquest for Edith Wilson's death had been on the same day as the dinner, and the verdict had been given as death by accidental overdose. No one had suspected any foul play, up until then. Everyone in the family agreed that Edith had been getting increasingly absentminded with age, and it was quite possible that she could have taken an overdose of her prescription Veronal. Even the doctor, who took the stand at the inquest, said that the autopsy had shown, that a little over twice the usual dosage had been ingested and that it was likely that Edith had made the fatal mistake herself, by forgetting that she had already taken her medicine and repeating the dose.

Then at this dinner, after the inquest, the child Adelaide made this alarming declaration that she saw someone put something in Edith's bedtime glass of milk. When prompted to give out the name of the person she had allegedly seen, meddling with the fateful glass of milk, she did some play acting and said she couldn't reveal the name because *she liked this person and didn't want to get this person into trouble.* At the time, no one took the child's babbling seriously because she often spoke wildly, had an over developed imagination, and constantly did and said things to get unnecessary attention. But after she wound up dead, suddenly she had everyone's attention because the people in the house realised that whoever had killed Edith, had taken the child's declaration seriously enough to have killed her too, and consequently must've been *someone whom the child knew well and had been at the dinner table that night.'*

'Who all were there, exactly, at dinner that night?' Jeremy asked.

'The entire family and two neighbours. Family members included Judge Wilson, John Griffin, Timothy, Evelyn and Antonio Baloney...,

'Just curious, is their last name really Baloney?' Rachel asked, unable to suppress the hint of a smile.

'Well, it's some Italian name like that. It's spelt B-e-l-l-o-n-i.'

Jeremy spoke up, 'Ah, Belloni! That would make him Antonio Belloni – he is quite well known, Inspector. Quite the celebrity in racing circles.'

'Baloney, Beelloni – sounds about same to me. All I know is that he's Italian and I can't pronounce foreign names too well.'

'That's alright, Inspector, so getting back to the fateful dinner table, you were saying...'

'Yes. That night, the family members included the Judge, his daughter Evelyn, the husband Antonio, the son - young Timothy Wilson, John Griffin and the child Adelaide. The only outsiders at the dinner were their neighbours, Henry Cavendish and his wife, Sofia. The problem was that, we couldn't zero in on anybody because all their alibis checked out, at the time that the child had supposedly drowned.'

What were their alibis?' Rachel asked.

'Well, although Judge Wilson wasn't really on our list of suspects, given that Adelaide is his daughter, we still checked everyone's whereabouts, around the time the child had drowned, just to be sure. The Judge had been at the yacht club all morning, where he met up and played bridge with some friends. His son, Timothy Wilson, went for sailing practice with a group of other young men. Several people saw them. Captain John Griffin and Antonio Baloney were at the garage, teetering about with Antonio's Alfa Romeo. The garage boy says they were there all morning and only went out of his sight when they went to the pub, for a beer or two. The bartender vouches that they came in together, had a couple of pints and then left together.'

'That still leaves Evelyn Belloni, Sofia and Henry Cavendish. Where were they?' Jeremy asked.

'Oh yes. Evelyn was at the hairdressers getting her weekly hairdo and all the rest of it – things women keep getting done, to fix their faces and other parts from deteriorating. She must have required a great deal of fixing because the woman at the beauty salon said, she was there all morning,' the inspector said, tongue-in-cheek, before continuing, 'Henry Cavendish took the early morning train to London. The conductor remembers him getting on the train, and his London club records checked out too. His wife, Sofia, kept to her usual routine of sleeping in till noon and the staff at Falcon's Crest vouches for her presence in the house, through the better part of the day. None of these people could have killed Adelaide, and yet each of them could have easily killed Edith Wilson, a week before that!'

'So, that leaves us right where we started,' Inspector Parker said, wearily.

'I'm afraid it does,' was Inspector Thomas' reply.

Chapter Four

Constable Goole poked his head into the Inspector's room and said, 'They've been brought in Sir... the boating party. What would you like me to do with 'em?'

'Well, Constable, you could take them out for sightseeing and some Devonshire cream teas. What do you think you're supposed to do with them?' Inspector Thomas asked him, in a dangerously polite voice.

'Well, Sir... I'm not sure...' Constable Goole was not allowed to finish his sentence.

'Bring them in here, for Pete's sake!' the inspector boomed.

But before he could respond, a well dressed young man brushed past the Constable rudely and said, 'I say. What's all this? Why have we been hauled off my yacht, and brought in here, like a pack of criminals, Inspector? I demand an explanation!'

'And you'll get one! Where are the others? Ask them all to come in,' Inspector Thomas told him curtly.

'It's going to get awfully crowded in here. Would you like us to wait outside?' Inspector Parker asked him politely.

'Not at all, the more the merrier. Besides, the Superintendent seems to think that you lot, have a better chance of solving this case than we do. I don't want anyone going back and tattling to him that I'm withholding precious information and hampering your razor sharp detecting abilities,' Inspector Thomas retorted, with a degree of sarcasm. The animosity was suddenly out in the open, and obvious to everyone in the room. It made everyone uncomfortable.

Inspector Parker spoke up, in his usual quiet way and said, 'I'm sure the Superintendent's only intention was to provide you with some additional backup. I would welcome it, if I were you, in a complicated case like this. Let's not forget, that we're on the same side, Thomas.'

'Right! Of course, we'll get on with it then,' Inspector Thomas said, in a bluff manner, ignoring the olive branch extended by his colleague.

As the four young people walked in, Rachel suddenly jumped up and squealed with delight, 'Helen Cavendish! Why I never! Imagine bumping into you - here of all places. I never thought the 'Miss Cavendish', the inspector was talking about, would turn out to be you.'

'Why Rachel Markham - you dark horse. What on earth are you doing here? It's lovely to see you. Goodness, it's been ages. How have you been?' Helen said, as she walked up and gave Rachel a tight hug.

'I take it, that you two young ladies know each other?'Inspector Thomas asked.

'Of course, we know each other! This girl, here, is a certified bosom friend of mine. We were best friends at school, and then both of us were packed off, during the war, to the same finishing school in Switzerland, which was such a lark really, wasn't it, Helen?' Rachel chuckled.

'Absolutely cent percent true!' Helen giggled back.

'Helen darling, I'd like you to meet my husband – Jeremy,' Rachel told her friend.

This time Helen squealed, 'I don't believe it. You're married? And I don't even know about it? Hello, Jeremy. Why wasn't I invited? I ought to have been the maid-of-honor! Did you two run off and get married?'

Jeremy replied, sardonically, 'I wish we had, with all the fuss people make when one gets married, but sadly, no.'

Rachel piped up, 'Oh, Helen, we had this beautiful tiny white wedding, in a tiny church near my Uncle Charles' home in the country. And I did send you an invite, at your father's house in London, but I suppose you never got it.'

Helen said, 'You suppose right. Wild horses wouldn't have kept me away, if I had. That house was blitzed in the war, ages ago. He bought a place up here in Dartmouth, after that. And I've been traveling through Italy and Spain and just got back here myself. I did go to your house in Kensington to look for you, when I was passing through London, on my way back from the continent. But the people living there, said that your folks had sold the place and moved to the country, over a year ago, and that they had no forwarding address.'

'Oh, yes. It's a long story and we'll have a good old chinwag like the old times, and I'll fill you up on everything. Darling! I've missed you. We have so much catching up to do!' Rachel said, her eyes shining with happiness.

At this point, Jeremy spoke up and said to Rachel, 'My dear, I hate to interrupt your wonderful reunion, but the Inspector is trying to conduct an investigation here.'

Helen spoke up in Rachel's defence, 'So sorry. It's just so much fun meeting your long lost best friend, out of the blue. But we'll behave ourselves, won't we Rachel?'

'We'll certainly try!'Rachel said, as both the girls broke out into laughter.

'Well, I'm glad at least someone's enjoying themselves, in this investigation,' Inspector Thomas grumbled and continued, 'Right then, I'll get straight to it. Mr. Baloney, do you recognise this man? We have reason to believe he is from Italy.'

Antonio Belloni who had been leaning against the wall, stood up straight as the Inspector addressed him, and came forward to see the picture the inspector was holding up in the air. Rachel observed that he was very handsome. *He has the face of Michaelangelo's David,* she thought to herself. He wore a tight white sailing tee shirt that accentuated his strong chiselled physique. He looked like an athlete and had the perfect tan that only someone, who spent a great deal of time under the Sun, could boast of. There was something about the way he moved, that gave Rachel the impression that he was dangerous and yet he looked like a poet. Perhaps it was his melting dark chocolate eyes, coupled with almost black ringlet curls that came down to his shoulders and framed his face artistically. He was an inch or two taller than Jeremy and from his full height he addressed the inspector in somewhat broken English.

'My name is not *Baloney*, Ispettore! I am *the* Antonio Belloni. You say to me, that this man is from Italy. So are many, many other people. That does not mean, I *riconoscere*... sorry how you say... recognise this person,' Antonio Belloni said, with a dramatic hand gesture.

'Er...yes, Mr. Beelloni. Are you sure you don't recognise him? Why don't you take a closer look?' The inspector prompted him.

Antonio Belloni drew himself up and replied indignantly, 'I am a race car driver, Ispettore! And I have the most perfect eyes. I see the picture, and no! I say, I do not know this person.'

Rachel smiled inwardly as she thought to herself, *I'll say - he certainly does have the 'most perfect eyes.'*

Helen's voice broke her reverie, as she exclaimed out loud, 'Oh, but I do! My stepmother and I were just talking about him this morning. He came up to us at the tearoom, the other day, and he was very drunk. He wanted Sofia's autograph but somehow through his drunken haze, he managed to recognise Captain John Griffin, who was with us that day. Perhaps you ought to ask him. I'm sure he'll know more about him.'

The inspector replied, 'Yes, the Captain was kind enough to stop by, at the station today, and he informed us about that encounter. It seems he was a deserter from one of the Captain's platoons. We now know that the man came to Dartmouth, with the specific objective of making his way to Ravenrock House, but we need to know why. It may throw some light on why he wound up dead. Are you sure you don't recognise him, Mr. *Beelloni?*'

Timothy Wilson spoke up, in an irritated tone, 'Look here now, Inspector. He's already told you he doesn't. Twice. So I'd put a lid on it, if I were you.'

Evelyn Belloni spoke up for the first time. Her voice was soft, yet clear as a bell. She addressed her brother with a certain indulgence, 'Do calm down, Timothy. I'm sure the Inspector has his reasons.' Then turning to the Inspector she asked, 'Might I ask, why you think, my husband has anything to do, with this man coming here, Inspector?'

Rachel turned to observe Evelyn. She was petite, and a very dainty and pretty young woman. She had delicate features and a head full of shingled dark hair that was done up fashionably in tiny tight curls. With her slightly upturned nose and big blue eyes, she reminded Rachel, of 'Tinker Bell' in the illustrated Peter Pan books, one read as a child.

'Because, Mrs. *Beelloni,* we think the victim came here from Italy. We found some Italian currency in his wallet, and we are also quite certain that the man came here specifically to meet someone at Ravenrock, possibly on someone's express invitation. He was carrying the address *with clear directions to the house,* on him. And since your husband is the only Italian in your family, one assumes...' The inspector was not allowed to finish, as Evelyn cut in.

'Well, my husband and I certainly didn't invite him over, Inspector and from what I hear; it seems perfectly obvious that John didn't either. Perhaps you can ask our Father, if he knows anything about it,' Evelyn told him. There seemed to be a certain finality and strength in her voice that conveyed to the Inspector that she would not allow him to badger her husband any longer.

Rachel looked upon her in admiration, as she realised, how subtly she had manipulated the situation, without any fuss, to the outcome she desired, and no one else had noticed.

'Yes. Well. Good idea. I think we'll do just that,' was the inspector's reply.

'Is there anything else?' Evelyn asked him sweetly.

'Not for now, but I'd request you all to stay on dry land, for a while. We may need your help, to take this further.'

Timothy answered, 'Right. That's doable I suppose.'

As the party of four left the room, Rachel too excused herself, and joined Helen outside the Station.

Helen introduced her to her neighbours; Timothy, Evelyn and Antonio. After the informal introductions were over and pleasantries exchanged, they decided to take a walk along the quay before lunching at the cafe.

As the Bellonis and Timothy walked slightly ahead, Helen and Rachel fell back from others to talk.

'So, where are you and Jeremy putting up?' Helen asked Rachel, linking her arm with Rachel's.

'At a small hotel, just down the road,' Rachel said, pointing ahead, in the direction of the hotel.

'Not anymore, you aren't, because I am officially abducting you and your husband, and moving your things to Falcon's Crest today. We have plenty of room, and the place is simply crawling with staff, cooks, maids and so on... so, you won't be a bother. And, you will simply love Sofia. Besides, I will not take no, for an answer!' Helen informed her, with a determined nod.

'Who is this Sofia? How come, I don't remember her at all?' Rachel asked puzzled.

'Because Sofia Burnett is Daddy's latest wife. You know, the actress,' Helen replied with a smile.

'Oh that is news! And how very exciting it must be, for you, to have someone that famous, living in the house. Unless of course, she's a tantrum throwing demon at home,' Rachel grinned.

'No, she's lovely.'

'Is she very glamorous?'

'Oh, yes. Very.'

'Must be interesting, for you to have someone like that, for a stepmum.'

'I was worried at first, when he told me that he had gone and gotten married again. I think he ends up proposing, everytime there's a lull in the conversation with one of his girlfriends. But I can tell you, she is a distinct improvement over the last two!' Helen said, as the two girls broke out into laughter.

Chapter Five

The next morning dawned bright and sunny with a pleasant, cool summer breeze blowing across the glittering River Dart. At Falcon's Crest, Sofia Burnett awoke early as the sun shone in through her bedroom window, delivering pools of light on and around her bed. She got up, saw that it was a beautiful day and decided to join Helen and her new houseguests, Jeremy and Rachel, on the terrace for a spot of breakfast. It was far too beautiful a day, to stay cooped up indoors. She put on her dressing gown and headed towards the stairs, where she met her French maid, Marie, coming down.

'Good morning, Madame. Shall I bring your morning coffee to your boudoir?' Marie said, somewhat surprised to see her mistress up and about so early.

'I'd like it on the terrace, for a change, Marie. Please bring it over there.'

'Oui, Madame', Marie said, before heading towards the kitchen, to prepare the fresh brew, her mistress coveted.

As she walked upstairs to the deck, Sofia heard the sound of laughter. She walked through the large glass enclosed seating area - that also housed a telescope for a closer look at the panoramic views surrounding them on all sides. The space was furnished in an ultra modern fashion. This was Henry Cavendish's sanctum in the house and he had especially shipped in the famous interior decorator 'Oswald' from New York to design it. The room had been showcased in several design journals in America. Sofia didn't like it much, as she found it far too modern for her comfort. She preferred her own sitting room on the ground floor that was furnished with beautiful antiques and cheerful chintz sofas. It had high ceilings, a classic stone fireplace and French windows overlooking the garden.

On the other hand, Henry's minimalistic space consisted of two spectacularly designed twenty-seater cream leather sofas, shaped as semi circles, facing one another. The sofas circled a large round fireplace, created with polished black wood and stone, set dramatically in the middle of the room, with a copper chimney above it. There was a copper and glass bar counter with hand sculpted designer barstools, at one end of the room. A large gramophone and wireless set stood next to it. On the other side of the room, a cream coloured grand piano, imported all the way from Hollywood in America, stood alone. It was a celebrity by itself and had been used by Ira and George Gershwin for a famous Hollywood musical, featuring Fred Astaire, in the early 30s. The piano had been Henry Cavendish's wedding gift to Sofia. Other than that, the room was clear.

She walked the length of the room and went through the open glass door on the other side, which connected to the terrace. She found Helen, Rachel and Jeremy seated under a large white canopy, around the glass topped table, leisurely enjoying a laid back breakfast. Rachel was saying something amusing, in her usual animated fashion, while Helen threw her head back and laughed. Sofia smiled at their camaraderie. It invoked a memory of an idyllic scene, from a painting she had once seen at the Louvre.

'Good morning. What a glorious day!' She greeted them, as she approached the table.

'It certainly is. Good morning, Sofia. Would you like some tea?' Rachel offered with a smile, as Sofia sank into the cushions of a chair, next to her.

'Never touch the stuff, my dear. Reminds me of ditch water. I'll stick to my usual cup of strong black coffee, thank you. Spruces one up. And God knows, I could do with some sprucing up today.' Sofia told her.

'Yes, you are up rather early, darling. Didn't you sleep well last night?' Helen asked Sofia.

'Like a baby. You know, I have no idea why people say sleeping early and rising early helps. If you ask me, it makes my eyes go all puffy. Nothing like staying up late and getting up late for that all special glow, I always say!'

'Ah! Finally, my wife has found a true compatriot!' Jeremy said, with a smile.

'Your wife is a smart woman, Jeremy. Remarkable, really, to see such horse sense, in someone so young.' Sofia told Jeremy, with a grin in Rachel's direction.

'Being complimented this early in the morning, always helps me attain my all special glow,' Rachel laughed.

At that moment, Sofia's French maid Marie walked up to the table with Sofia's black coffee service and said to her, 'Madame, there is a telephone call for a Monsieur Richards in the foyer.'

As Sofia looked at her uncomprehendingly, Jeremy pushed his chair back and got up, 'That would be for me, thank you. If you'll excuse me ladies, I must take the call. It's probably Inspector Parker.'

Rachel said, 'Yes, darling. Go ahead.' As Jeremy left, Rachel turned to Sofia and said, 'Hmm. The smell of freshly brewed coffee is so intoxicating! May I have some?'

'Of course, honey. Marie, please bring another demitasse and serve Madame some fresh coffee.' Sofia instructed her maid.

As Marie left to bring more coffee, Helen turned to Rachel and said, 'So, what do you propose we do today, Rachel? After breakfast, I mean.'

'I was hoping to go for a swim at the sandy cove I spotted day before. I think it's quite close from here,' Rachel answered.

Helen said, 'That's a capital idea! It's a perfect day for a swim. We'll head down as soon as we're ready.'

Sofia asked, 'Oh, you don't mean the cove below? But, that's where that girl, Adelaide, drowned.'

'Really?' Rachel asked, intrigued.

'Yes and what's more, we are all suspects because the cove belongs to us. Oh! It was a ghastly affair,' Sofia said, reminiscing.

Rachel said, 'You mean that cove is part of the Falcon's Crest estate? I did see the sign that said 'private' but had no idea it belonged to you.'

'Yes, the cove is part of the grounds. Daddy bought the place because of it. He's rather proud of having his own little private cove and a boathouse. There are steps leading down to it from here. I'll show you.' Helen told her.

Sofia wasn't sure. She asked, 'Are you sure it's safe, honey? I mean, that girl was drowned there only recently. What if there's a lunatic about, who likes to go around drowning girls?'

Helen replied, 'Oh, Sofia! I sincerely doubt that. I think Adelaide went and drowned herself.'

'What makes you think that?' Rachel asked Helen.

'Well, she didn't know how to swim and must've been practicing swimming secretly and probably panicked that she had swum out too far. She was a stupid, spoilt child.'

'That's a cruel thing to say, honey. I'll admit, it was a tad ghoulish, the way she gloated on about how she knew who had killed her aunt, but wouldn't give out the name of the person. Almost, as if, she was enjoying the experience, of seeing someone squirm in their seat. I didn't take her seriously of course, at the time, but it is obvious now that she did know, or worse, pretended to know who murdered her aunt. The awful thing was that Edith had been like a mother to that ungrateful child. Anyhow, we mustn't speak ill of the dead, my dear,' Sofia said to Helen, with an uncharacteristic display of compassion.

'That's just superstition, Sofia! Fact is, everyone around here knew she was a cunning little thing, in her own stupid way. But I still can't believe anyone in their right mind, would kill a child, however horrible she may have been. Though, I wouldn't put it past her, to try and learn swimming on her own, just so she could show off her skills to everyone later,' Helen said.

'But it seems like too much of a coincidence, my dear! Her insinuations that she knew the killer, and then winding up dead, the very next day! I somehow agree with the others. I think some unhinged person may have actually drowned the child. And if that is the case, it may not be a bright idea for you girls to go swimming about... at least until he's caught.' Sofia concluded, looking concerned.

'Don't worry, Sofia, Helen was the captain of our swim team back at school. She's one of the strongest swimmers. I know. I very much doubt anyone will succeed in drowning her.' Rachel told Sofia jocularly.

'That's right and if by chance there is some lunatic about, I'd like to see him try any funny business with us, eh, Rachel? We'll show him a thing or two about drowning people!' Helen quipped back.

At that moment, Jeremy came back and questioned Rachel, 'Sounds like you charming ladies are busy hatching nefarious schemes. Exactly, who, are you planning to drown, darling?'

Rachel answered with a smile, 'Oh never mind that Jeremy, did you know that secret cove of ours, actually belongs to them?'

Jeremy responded, 'Interesting! At least, I can rest easy now, knowing that you won't be trespassing on someone else's private property.'

Sofia said, 'That's the least of our worries. If the girls insist on going swimming there, I'm afraid, I'll have to get ready and join them later. I am responsible for you while your father is away, you know.'

'I hardly need chaperoning, Sofia. Besides, we'll have the long arm of the law, protecting us as well. Jeremy will be joining us too, won't you?' Helen asked, looking expectantly at Jeremy.

Jeremy replied, 'I'm afraid, I can't. I have some bad news. The inspector called to say that your neighbour, Captain John Griffin, was in a car accident this morning. Apparently, someone cut the brakes in the Alfa Romeo and almost succeeded in killing him.'

Helen sprang up, shattering the cup and saucer that fell from her hand, onto the terrace floor, as she exclaimed, 'Oh, my God! John. No! How is he now? Where is he? I must go to him.'

'He's alright. Luckily for him, a tree came in the way while he was hurtling downhill and stopped the car before it could go over the cliff. He's had a narrow escape. And all he has to show for it, are a few bad bruises and a broken leg. They've taken him to the Cottage Hospital, and the inspector has asked me to join him there. You can all come along with me, if you want to see him.'

Sofia spoke up, as if coming out of a daze, 'My God! There really is a lunatic about. And from the looks of it, he's trying to wipe out the family up at Ravenrock one by one.'

Chapter Six

Captain John Griffin lay trussed up in the hospital bed with his right leg suspended up in a cast. He was feeling rather sorry for himself. It was especially in times like this that he missed his late wife, Pamela, enormously. They had met under extraordinary circumstances, at the onset of the Second World War. Amidst the madness that surrounded them at the time; they had found solace in each other's arms. It had been an irresistible affair. She had been a beautiful young nurse, stationed at London, and he had been a dashing young Captain. The passionate affair that resulted from their constant meeting had led to the inevitable and Pamela had found herself three months pregnant. Although he had not given marriage much thought before that, John felt duty bound to marry young Pamela much against her father, Judge Wilson's wishes. Judge Wilson, on the other hand, was convinced that John was a rake and a scoundrel of the first order who had cheated his naive young daughter into an immoral union.

A few months after the registry, John had been called to the front. The fighting had started in earnest. It was only after John left his heavily pregnant wife behind and went to war, that the Judge finally came to his senses and accepted their wedlock. He traveled to London and pleaded with Pamela to come home to the safety of Dartmouth. By then, Pamela had given birth to her daughter Anne and London was being blitzed with frightening regularity. The Judge succeeded in convincing Pamela in moving to his house in Dartmouth for the sake of his granddaughter Anne's safety. Ironically, Pamela and Anne had survived the London Blitz only to get killed in the Torquay bombing in May 1944.

John had since heard the whole story time and again from Pamela's aunt, Edith and Pamela's little sister, Adelaide. And it had formed a vivid picture in his mind.

Edith and he had spoken about the fateful day many times. In 1944, the ongoing war made for a gloomy atmosphere and gave very little scope for fun, especially for little children. Most of the lodgings in and around Dartmouth had been billeted for soldiers. In preparation for D-Day landings in June and, in the months leading up to D-Day, thousands of American army personnel had arrived with the 3204th Quartermaster Service Company billeted in and around Torquay, Chelston and Cockington.

Pamela had thought it would brighten things up considerably for them to visit Aunt Edith's house in Torquay for the weekend. Apart from being very fond of

Aunt Edith, she had been looking forward to seeing her little sister Adelaide again, who lived with Aunt Edith. Perched atop a hill, Aunt Edith's house – Glendale, had a beautiful view of Torquay. Despite the restrictions on public movement in the countryside, Pamela and her three year old daughter Anne had managed to get a ride from Dartmouth upto Brixham, from where a local boatman ferried them across to Torquay. After an early lunch, Aunt Edith and Adelaide had gone to their rooms to take their afternoon naps and Pamela had made herself comfortable in the sitting room at Glendale, which was strewn with Anne's toys. After this, John could only surmise what had taken place. Pamela had survived for a few more hours and had related the incident to her Aunt Edith before she finally succumbed to her injuries at the hospital. In his mind's eye, he could see how the events had unfolded.

It had happened at three in the afternoon. Tired after their trip and Aunt Edith's sparse yet delicious fare at luncheon, Pamela had fallen asleep on the settee. Three year old Anne had continued playing silently with her toys, when she heard the buzzing sound. Anne hardly knew her father, since he had been away, fighting in the war, ever since she was born. She had clung to her mother instinctively for warmth and safety that only a loving parent can provide. The noise was confusing for her. She wanted to run to her mother but she was also curious. She looked back once more at her sleeping mother. Suddenly the sound became deafening – a buzz that sounded like a thousand angry hornets magnified a hundred times. By then the noise had woken Pamela and she saw little Anne standing on her tiptoes, her chubby little hands parting the lace curtains to see what it was all about. By the time Pamela could reach her, it was too late. Anne had stood mesmerised; her blue eyes wide open as twenty one Fokker aircrafts came in to the Bay.

Glendale House was at a height on the edge of the cliff and she saw one of the planes come close, so close that she could even see the face of the pilot just before he released the 1000 pound bomb into the Bay along with the others. Before Pamela could get them both out of harm's way, machine gun bullets sprayed the side of the house. The glass shattered, and the old roof above them caved in from the shelling, and both mother and daughter were buried under the debris. The blast of bombs in the Bay below drowned out their screams. It had all happened in minutes. Though the sitting room at Glendale was reduced to rubble, the rest of the house remained miraculously intact and Edith and Adelaide, whose rooms were towards the back of the house, had survived the air attack.

The Fokker planes left, after having dropped their bombs into the empty bay - which only hours before had been the anchorage for a naval fleet - thousand strong, preparing for the epic battle of Normandy. The following day, the fleet returned and commenced the loading of the troops for the Normandy invasion. John knew that during Operation Overlord, more than 23,000 men of the American 4th Infantry Division departed Torquay Harbour slipways for Utah Beach. Five thousand had died within one month. They had landed at Utah losing close to 200 men.

Anne and her mother, Pamela had gone down in history as an insignificant percentage of collateral damage in the wake of World War II. They had taken a part of John's heart with them.

He heard the news from the war office and came to Dartmouth, as soon as he was released eight months after the Torquay bombing. The day he came to Dartmouth, to meet Judge Wilson face to face, was also clearly etched in his memory. He had wanted to visit the graves of his wife and child, nearby, and mustered up the courage to finally meet his father-in-law.

He remembered the day, as if it were yesterday. It had been the middle of January, and bitterly cold winds blew across from the choppy seas. John had walked up the steep path from the Darthaven Marina to Ravenrock. He had been carrying his army supply holdall on his left shoulder. He remembered pausing to take a few deep breaths. His breath steamed up in front of his face as he looked up. From the point in the path he had seen the shingles of the old house through the trees, and the statuesque almost black-brown slanting roof that stood out dramatically against the slate grey skies. It gave him a feeling of foreboding but he continued to walk up, until, a few steps later the house came into full view. The old Tudor house looked as if it had been freshly renovated and painted. The garden was well kept and despite the cold, the flower beds were in full bloom. From there on the scene played on like a motion picture in his mind.

He remembered walking up to the main entrance and using the big brass knocker shaped like a lion's head, to announce his arrival. As the chill wind continued to blow across the hilltop, he had shivered and waited for what seemed like an interminable amount of time. The door was finally opened by an elderly lady in her 60s. She had short, waving salt and pepper hair, a weather beaten yet pleasing face and was dressed simply in a grey wool skirt and a black cardigan.

'Yes?' She had asked suspiciously. There had been too many ex-army fellows going door-to-door collecting money for some fund or the other, or trying to sell things, in the past month or so.

'I'm here to meet Judge Wilson. He's not expecting me but if you could kindly tell him that Captain John Griffin is here to see him, I'm sure he will see me,' then after a pause, he added, 'I am his son-in-law.'

The old lady's eyes widened in surprise and she fluttered in excitement, 'Oh, but we thought you had died in the war. Oh, my God, John Griffin! Of course, do come in. Where are my manners? I am Pamela's aunt, Edith, Judge Wilson's sister. Please do come in. It's awfully cold.'

'Thank you,' he had said simply, as he walked in, and she closed the door behind him.

'Here, let me take your coat. My brother is in the study. I am so sorry about your terrible loss. Such a tragedy. Anne was a delightful child. And Pamela had always been the apple of his eye. Marcus took it very badly indeed. He never quite got over losing both Pamela and Anne at the same time. I'm sure, it was very hard on you too. In a way, it's a relief you are here. Perhaps, it will help him to have you here... to have someone close, to remember them by. Look at me, going on and on. You must think me quite mad. But it is quite a shock, you know, seeing you for the first time, but I do feel, as though I know you already.

Pamela spoke quite a lot about you.' As she chatted on, he had remained silent with a slight smile.

'You will want to meet Marcus, of course. Come with me,' she had beckoned, and led the way.

John remembered that he had found himself thinking, *so, Marcus is Judge Wilson's first name.* It sounded strange to his ears somehow. And even stranger, was the fact that he had not known his father-in-law's first name. Pamela always called him daddy and all her legal documents, before they married, read as, Pamela Wilson, daughter of Judge M Wilson.

John was lost in his own thoughts. Edith and he had walked in silence, through a dimly lit hallway into a comfortably furnished sitting room, where a crackling log fire was burning. The fire had looked inviting. Edith motioned him to sit down on an armchair near the fire. 'Please wait here. I must prepare him for this. He is frail and has, only recently, been diagnosed with a weak heart,' she had said, with kindness, before leaving the room.

He nodded and sat down on a leather armchair. Head bowed, hands entwined on his lap, he stared at the fire and waited patiently, as Edith went in to a door at the end of the main hall to announce his arrival to the father-in-law he had never met before. He wondered what he would be like. He had no idea how he would react to his son-in-law showing up at his doorstep. The Judge had refused to give his blessing when the marriage took place. He wondered, if he had forgiven him by this time. In all fairness to the Judge's sentiments, Pamela had been three months pregnant and carrying Anne when she married her lover. And Judge Wilson had viewed the affair, and the consequent marriage to a man with no known antecedents, as his daughter's greatest folly, and had refused to bless the union. However, a lot of water had flown under the bridge since and it was apparent to John from what Edith had told him, that in the end, the old man had not only forgiven his daughter but had fallen in love with the child she bore.

John didn't have to wait very long. A few minutes later, the man himself appeared in the doorway. He was about 5'9", with a portly build. Dressed in a navy blue blazer over dark grey wool trousers, he had a dignified air about him. He had a pleasant face like his sister, Edith. John could see the strong family resemblance and his bald head gave him a wizened appearance. He looked every inch the retired judge. And as he scrutinized John through his pince-nez, John got the curious feeling that there was nothing remotely weak about the man, irrespective of what his sister had given him to believe.

'Hello.' Judge Wilson said simply and held out his hand, as John got to his feet to accept his handshake. His grip was firm and strong.

Edith excused herself, to give them some privacy and ostensibly to get some refreshment.

Both men took stock of each other. There was a degree of wariness despite the outward cordiality.

'So, you are alive, after all?' Judge Wilson remarked.

John was tempted to say *'Last time I checked, I certainly was'* but stopped himself with an inward smile. Aloud, he answered with a simple 'Yes.'

'And I suppose, you've come here now, to claim your wife's inheritance?' Judge Wilson asked, matter-of-factly.

John was taken aback with his blatant rudeness. 'I wasn't aware she had one. I came here to give you this,' he said, bending down to take a manila packet out of his holdall.

The packet contained some faded pictures and a bunch of letters. John took out some pictures and handed them over to the Judge. The corners of the pictures were yellowed, frayed and bent, as if they had gone on a long journey with the owner. The first one Judge Wilson saw, was one of Pamela holding baby Anne in her arms. It must have been taken soon after the baby's christening because little Anne was swaddled in a christening gown. Another one, was a picture of eighteen year old Pamela in her nurse's uniform just before she married. She had a clear gaze, and was looking straight at the camera, with a slight smile on her face. There was one of her as a bride, wearing a simple knee length white dress, and a white hat, holding a spray of lilies. She looked beautiful, as she laughed into the camera. Judge Wilson sat down on the other armchair, looked up at John and said, 'Why now? Why after all this time?'

'The war taught me many things, Judge. One of the most important things it taught me, was that blood is indeed thicker than water, and that although I went to war, and saw thousands of men dying around me, the news of my family's loss was the saddest thing I have ever had to bear. So you see, I know how you must feel. We shared the same family and bear the same cross. I thought I owed it to you, to share some of my treasures with you. It seemed greedy, not to.'

'What about you? Don't you want these pictures anymore?' Something in the Judge's tone suggested offence and John decided that his coming all the way to meet the man had been a waste of time since it looked as though the Judge still bore a deep seated grudge against him.

'The war may have kept me away from my daughter, for the most part, but I have more happy memories than you could count, Judge, with my wife. If you don't want these, I'll take them with me,' he said getting up, his face an inscrutable mask. He held his hand out to retrieve his family's pictures and said 'I am sorry I came unannounced. And now, if you will excuse me, I will catch the next ferry out.'

The Judge's face fell. Instinctively he realised that he had overstepped a fine line with this young man. He apologized, 'I am sorry if I've been very rude. Forgive me. It seems to me you've come a long way just to meet me. The war has made me a wary man. And an old one. Do at least stay for a few days.'

'I don't wish to impose...' John hesitated.

Edith spoke from the doorway, as she came in holding a tray with some tea and homemade scones. 'Nonsense! You must stay with us. You are family now. There is so much we need to talk about. Pamela loved you, and I can't speak for Marcus, but I, for one, want to get to know you better. Besides, Adelaide, Pamela's little sister, will be home from school any moment now, and she would be crushed, if she didn't get to meet you.'

John had found himself saying, 'You are very kind, Edith. Thank you. I too, would like to meet the whole family, and get to know you all better. Pamela was very fond of you and Adelaide. Her letters were full of amusing stories about Adelaide and Glendale.' John smiled for the first time since he had entered their house. And before he knew it, his weeklong visit had turned into an extended two year stay.

Chapter Seven

The hospital room was crowded, and Rachel felt rather out of place. She didn't know Captain John Griffin at all, and had simply joined Jeremy, Helen and Sofia mainly because she didn't want to be left behind on her own at Falcon's Crest, and out of a sense of curiosity. Helen's reaction to the news had surprised her. She didn't know that the two families were so close. Soon after they reached the hospital, Jeremy was called away by Inspector Parker, to pay an official police visit on Judge Wilson at Ravenrock House. And once Jeremy had left, Rachel felt as if she was intruding on an intimate family reunion. Antonio Belloni and Timothy Wilson got up from the chairs, as the ladies walked in, and the patient himself had greeted Helen and Sofia enthusiastically as they entered. Rachel felt a tad awkward, and stood back to observe as both Helen and Sofia went to embrace John.

Sofia reached first and said, 'We came as soon as we heard. Oh, John! What a scare you gave us! How are you feeling, honey?'

Helen spoke up, 'How awful of you, and how could you do this to us, John! You terrible man... you scared us to death.'

John was amused. 'Wait a minute! I'm the one, who almost got killed. I'm the one you are supposed to be feeling sorry for, and all you can come up with is that I scared you! Women! Who can understand them?'

Sofia retorted, 'Oh, you are a terrible man, but thank goodness you are alive!'

Helen asked, 'What were you doing, gadding about in the Alfa Romeo anyway?'

'It's not, as though, I knew someone had cut the brakes, and was on a suicide mission you know. I just took the old girl for a spin, and the next thing I know I was going like the wind, completely out-of-control, and couldn't stop.'

'Yes, yes, but what were you doing in the Alfa Romeo? It's Antonio's car!'

'Look, the weather was gorgeous, and I just felt, this overwhelming need, to be out, driving around, the wind in my hair, and all that sort of thing. I used the last of my petrol ration and I wanted to make the most of it. Lucky for him, I did, or it could have been him or worse, Evelyn, and we all know how she drives! I think it was a lucky break, for all of us, that it was me behind the wheel. And that I had the intelligence, to drive it into a tree, to stop it.'

'You smart boy. I didn't know you did that on purpose!'

'Of course, I did. As much as I admire the River Dart, I had no intention of plunging into it, along with the car. Besides, Antonio would have never forgiven me, for drowning his Alfa Romeo! Isn't that right, Antonio?'

'I am sorry... what is it you say?' Asked Antonio, who had been staring at Rachel, with undiluted admiration in his eyes, in a way that only the Italian male can pull off, without seeming rude, when they see beauty. He turned towards John.

John repeated, 'I was just telling these wonderful ladies, that you would have never forgiven me, had I let the Alfa Romeo go into the river!'

Antonio shrugged his shoulders and said, 'she is beautiful, yes, but she is ...how you say? She is just an automobile. I can replace her but I thank Santa Maria, for saving you, my friend. I also see, you have not met Helen's beautiful friend.'

At that moment, Sofia noticed that Rachel was still standing near the door, blushing beetroot red, unused to the blatant admiration that Antonio was conferring upon her. Sofia quickly moved to correct this social gaff and introduced her to John. 'I'm sorry, we've been so busy scolding you that we forgot to make proper introductions... John, meet Rachel, an old school friend of Helen's, and Rachel, this is Captain John Griffin. And of course, you've already met Antonio at the police station,' she said, with an amused grin.

Antonio added with a charming smile, 'Bellissima, who can forget a girl, like the English rose...'

Rachel stepped forward and smiled brightly at him, 'You flatter me, Mr. Belloni,' then turning to John, she said politely, 'I'm very pleased to meet you, Captain Griffin.'

'Charmed, I'm sure, and don't mind Antonio. I have it on perfectly good authority, that Italian men are notorious flirts, in a completely harmless sort of way,' was John's amused response, as he tried to put Rachel at ease.

'Oh, it isn't that. It's just that, I'm afraid, I seem to have barged in, on a private moment,' Rachel responded with a chagrined smile.

'Not at all. It is very kind of you, to pay me a visit. I take it, that you are on holiday here?'

'Yes, well, I certainly am, but my husband is on a busman's holiday, actually.' Rachel replied tongue-in-cheek.

Helen explained, 'John, her husband is Jeremy Richards – the famous Scotland Yard detective, and they are helping the police solve this case. They are quite a team. You remember the Rutherford murder case, which was all over the papers, last year? They solved it. Isn't it exciting... To have first class detectives, on our side?

'I'll say! Now, I'm really very pleased, to meet you. I'd like to get my hands on the person, who is behind all this! Just wink at me, Rachel, and put me on to him, once you know 'whodunit', and I'll take it from there. No point in wasting all this army training, is there? I'll fix the chap, alright.'

Rachel laughed and said, 'I'm sure, we'd all prefer that you get well first.'

Helen chipped in, 'Yes, it's hard to imagine, you hobbling about on sticks, fixing people, at the moment!'

'I may be hobbling, for a while, my fair Helen, but I'm strong as an ox and shall be well armed with the aforementioned sticks!' John said, with a boyish smile, and then turning towards Rachel, he asked, 'I say, will it be possible for me to have a word with your husband? I do have something that is bothering me, well apart from broken bones and all that, that I'd like to share with him.'

'Yes, of course, that can be arranged, Captain Griffin.'

'John, please call me John.'

'Right, I shall inform him that you would like to meet him, John.'

At that moment, the nurse came in with a basin of hot water and a towel, and announced in a business-like fashion, 'visiting hours are over now, and it's time for the patient's sponge bath. If you could all step outside, please.'

Helen said, 'we'll be back to visit you soon. Meanwhile, enjoy your sponge bath, and I'd advise you to put any harebrained ideas, about using your sticks, away, and behave yourself, at least until, you get better!'

II

Meanwhile, in London, Henry Cavendish was alone in the doctor's waiting room, in Harley Street. The discreet brass plaque at the entrance read – Richard Farnon, MD. The doctor was an old friend of Henry's from his exuberant youth. In their bachelor days, they had spent quite a lot of time in each other's company. It seemed to Henry, that Richard was the only person, he could possibly confide in. He had tried getting in touch with him, immediately upon his arrival in London, but was told by the doctor's secretary that the doctor was away with his wife, in the south of France, on his annual, month-long holiday. Distraught, he had asked her when he was expected back, and was relieved to learn that he would be back, in the coming week. He had asked her to schedule an appointment for him, as soon as Richard was back.

The doctor's secretary was absent, and a slightly dim-witted young man, had let him in. The boy had looked at him blankly, and asked for his card. Henry gave it to him and informed him that he had an appointment. The boy showed him in to the waiting room, and after asking him to wait, left the room. Although, he was early for his appointment, Henry paced up and down, unused to being made to wait. A man in his position was used to people fawning over him, and over the years, special treatment was something he had come to take for granted. As with most, very successful people, his success had come at a cost – in his case, it had cost him his patience, along with an intense dislike and zero tolerance for inefficiency, especially in others. He wondered if the boy had even informed Richard of his arrival. In this case, he was even more impatient, as he was desperate to share his burden with Richard, the sooner, the better, and get some much needed advice.

Ten minutes went by like eternity and finally the inner door opened. He saw an enormous woman with a fox fur collar, exit from the doctor's chamber. As she floated by, regally, like a ship in full sail, he heard the doctor's buzzer go off, and saw the pale faced boy who had let him in, go into the chamber. The boy came out shortly and announced loudly, in to the air, as if the waiting room was full of people, 'Mister 'enry Cavendish.'

Henry grunted in acknowledgement, and went in.

'Good to see you, Henry. I'm sorry, that took so long.'

'Likewise, Dickie, old boy. I seem to recognise the woman who just left, but can't quite place her.'

'Oh, well, that was Mrs. Van Dyke - the Texan oil heiress.'

'Right, must've seen her picture in the papers. She seemed rather well-fed. What on earth was she visiting you about?'

'Now, Henry, telling you that, would be an inappropriate breach of doctor-patient confidentiality.' The doctor replied with a smile and asked, 'So, what can I help you with, today?'

'I have a rather delicate situation on hand, and I'm glad that you are strong on the confidentiality part, because I need your advice, on a rather tricky issue that's come up.'

'Go ahead, Henry. I can see that something has been bothering you, old boy. Although you look as good as ever, you've lost quite a lot of weight, since I saw you last.'

'That's probably because my wife - Sofia keeps putting me on those infernal diets – cabbage soup and fish and nonsense like that. But, yes, I am rather in a spot, of sorts, and didn't know what to do, so I came up to London to see you.'

'Well, it's evident that you are not here, for a health consultation, so go ahead, and spill the beans, Henry. Whatever it is, speak freely, you can rest assured that your secret will be safe with me.'

'Well, the thing is, Dickie ...,' he paused, trying to assemble his thoughts, and then blurted out, 'Sofia informed me two weeks ago, that she is pregnant.'

'Ah! I see.'

'Yes, I knew you would. I'm at my wit's end.'

'Is she absolutely certain? It could be a false alarm, you know.'

'Oh yes, she said that the local GP, over at Dartmouth, confirmed the 'good' news.'

'Does she know about...'

'No! We never spoke about it. It seemed unnecessary. I'm fifty four and she's forty. I never thought... I mean, I never even considered the possibility. And now, this happens.'

'Quite.'

Chapter Eight

Judge Wilson was seated in an armchair, in his study. He looked haggard. He missed his sister, Edith. She had been his friend and companion, ever since his wife, Dorothy, had died. She had been a selfless woman, and he had been very grateful that she had additionally taken over the responsibility of running his household, ever since she had moved in with him. He missed her comforting presence. It took the edge off living, surrounded by a lot of young people he couldn't quite understand, in a world that had gone mad during and after the War. Everything was so different now. The war had changed the old ways of life, irrevocably. First there was Edith's mysterious death. Then a week ago, some mad man had drowned his youngest daughter, Adelaide. Now, it looked, as though someone had tried to kill his son-in-law, John. The world, he felt was going to the dogs, and there was nothing he could do to prevent it. He felt lost and tired.

His daughter, Evelyn came into the study.

'I just got back from the Hospital, Daddy. Timothy and Antonio are still there with him. John was asking after you. He hoped you were alright. He specifically asked me to get back home and take care of you.'

'He's a good man. What are the doctors saying? Have the Police found out anything at all?'

'They say he was very lucky. He's got a few bruises and a broken leg, but that's about the extent of his injuries. It could have been a lot worse. It's a miracle he's alive. Thank God, the tree saved him from going over the cliff! The Police are still trying to find out what is going on here,' she said, as she sat down wearily, in an armchair near him.

Judge Wilson shook his head, 'Evelyn, my dear, I think I'm getting old. I can't understand what is going on anymore. People being poisoned, brakes being cut, young girls being drowned. Who would do things like that? This used to be such a safe haven. What I'd like to know is why the Police haven't caught the chap yet?'

'Yes, well Daddy, try not to upset yourself too much. Remember, the inspector is on his way and will be here anytime now to talk with you.'

'What's the good of talking to me? They ought to be out there, rounding up suspects. Like that deserter chap who was found drowned. What was he doing in these parts? What brought him here? They ought to be more alert. In my day, the Police were far more efficient. I wonder what the force is coming to these days.'

'Oh Daddy, I'm sure they are doing everything they can, to find out more. It's not as if they aren't doing anything. We're all upset about recent events, but it won't do any of us, any good, to point fingers at them, when it could just as easily, turn out to be, one of us.'

'My dear girl, whatever do you mean?'

'Oh, come now, Daddy. You don't suppose that Aunt Edith was killed by some roaming vagabond. Her milk was tampered with at home. And Adelaide being drowned right after, she claimed she knew who the killer was. The more I think about it, I get chills going up my spine, just to know, that it could be any one of us.'

Just then they heard the doorbell chime in the distance and Evelyn got up and said, 'that'll be the police. You will try and be agreeable?'

Judge Wilson sighed and said, 'Yes, dear, I always am. Bring them in here. And ask that new parlour maid, you hired, to bring some tea. Mine has gone quite cold.'

II

'Why! That is my sister Edith's handwriting. I'd recognise it anywhere. And you say, this was found on the drowned man?' Judge Wilson asked Inspector Thomas, who was accompanied by Inspector Parker and Jeremy Richards.

'Well, yes. It was found amongst his belongings, that were left behind, on dry land,' was the inspector's reply.

'Now, that is strange. I wonder what connection the man had with Edith, of all people.'

'Perhaps, she had asked him to visit the house, for some reason?'

'Yes, I see that, but why? I just don't understand. And how would she even know, someone like that? Unlike some women, Inspector, my sister led a rather quiet and sheltered life. Somehow, I find her interest in a young man of questionable antecedents like this, quite incomprehensible.'

'And yet, you are quite sure that the address and directions to Ravenrock house, on this paper, are in her handwriting?'

'Without a doubt, Inspector.'

'Are there any samples of Miss Edith's handwriting that we can compare this with?' Inspector Thomas asked the Judge.

'Of course, Inspector. You could take a look at the ledger, in which, she maintained house accounts. She ran this house, paid all the bills and took care of us all.'

'Thank you, Judge. I will ask the Sergeant to look into it immediately. Another thing, do you have any idea or suspicions, as to who would have a grudge against your sister?'

'Not that I'm aware of. As far as I know, my sister Edith hadn't an enemy in the world. Why would she? She was one of the nicest people you could meet. And I'm not just saying that because I was related to her. You can ask anyone who knew her, and they will probably tell you the same thing. As a Judge, I learnt a thing or two about human nature, and I can tell you this – Edith was a good human being and you'd have to go a long way, to find someone as selfless and kind as her.'

'Ahem. Yes of course. I don't doubt your word for a minute, Judge; however, it may help further the investigation if you could think of anyone, who may have felt otherwise. We must keep in mind, that someone hated her enough, to wilfully murder her.'

'Well. There was the old gardener that she dismissed from duty, about a month ago – Simon, I think his name was. But even so, I very much doubt that he would come back and murder her for being dismissed from gardening duties.'

'Yes. But we'll still follow up on his whereabouts and question him. I'll make a note of his name. My question however was, if anyone closer to home, had a grudge against her.'

'You mean in the family? That's preposterous. She was like a mother to them. She cared very deeply about this family, and was very protective about all the children. Especially, after my wife, Dorothy passed away. She was kindness itself. If the children did not go to pieces, after their mother died, it was only because Edith nurtured them the way their own mother would have and more so.

'Right, Sir. But there is the matter of her handwritten note being found on the dead man. There may be some events, or people, in her life, that you or the others in the family, were not aware of.'

'Yes, it certainly seems that way now. But it's still quite baffling. Really, I can't think why she would write to a man like that, and not tell me about it.'

'Did she seem normal, in the days leading up to her death? I mean, was there any change in her behaviour towards anyone? Did she seem anxious or worried?'

'Well, yes and no. She was not anxious, but she seemed to have renewed vigour. I did get a sense that she was enthusiastic about something, but I just presumed it had something to do, with her idea of setting up a hothouse to grow exotic flowers. She was very fond of gardening.'

At this point Jeremy spoke up and said, 'There is also the question of who would want to kill other members of your family. Can you think of anyone who has a grudge against the family or you in person?'

'Not a soul! Well, apart from the people I've sentenced, in the course of my duties, as a Judge. But I can tell you, that my judgements were entirely fair and evidence based, and I have a clear conscience, that I have never sent an innocent to the gallows.'

'Is there any case, you can remember, where someone may have felt unfairly punished? Or an instance, where any threat, was directed at you or your family. Please think, before you answer, Judge. This could be of vital importance.'

'I am sorry, but in the course of my long career, I can't remember anything like that.'

'Please do let us know, if you think of anything or remember any incident. Even the smallest thing sometimes can turn out to be, of immense importance in unravelling a case of this nature.'

'Wait! Now that you mention it, there was something long ago. Almost twenty years ago. But no, I don't suppose it will help. The people in question are long dead and gone. It can't have anything to do with, whatever it is, that is going on here.'

'Even so. Please enlighten us.'

'It is embarrassing, really. It was just some deranged young man, who was under the delusion that his wife was having an illicit affair with me, of all people! He came around to my house in London, waving a gun, and took a couple of pot shots at me. But he was put away, for attempted murder and consequently, died of tuberculosis in prison.'

'What about the lady in question?'

'Hardly a lady. She was an employee, a temporary secretary, who the typing firm had sent over, as a replacement to my long standing secretary - Mrs. Higgins. Now, what was her name... ah, yes, a Mrs. Lucy Jones – a saucy type of young woman. She had only been in my employ for a few months, when her drunken, trigger happy husband came by one evening, after she had left, and started shooting at me. I can tell you, I was more shocked than harmed by the incident.'

'What did you do?' Inspector Thomas asked the Judge, as Jeremy suppressed a smile. In his mind's eye, he could vividly imagine the scene. The drunken man taking pot shots, and the sober Judge jumping about the place, trying to avoid them.

'What else could I do? I hit the man with my walking stick, and my butler pushed him out the door. After which, we closed the door. The shooting had caused quite a commotion in the neighbourhood, and before I knew it, the Police arrived. He was booked for attempted murder, and consequently sentenced and sent to prison.'

'And what happened to his wife, this Mrs. Lucy Jones?'

'Last I heard, was that she committed suicide, shortly after the trial. I felt rather sorry for her, but there wasn't much I could do. Must've been fed up, of having to live her life, with such a foul tempered, obnoxious man for a husband.'

'Yes. Quite a tragedy. One last question Judge – about the alleged affair, this man accused you, of having with his wife. And please bear in mind, that we are all men of the world here, was there any truth in it?'

'An affair? With that sort of a woman? Of course not! Just because I said, I felt sorry for her, does not mean, that I was even remotely interested in her. As a man of the world, I hope you'll give me credit, for having better taste in women, Inspector. That woman, God rest her soul, was a common little thing, and I'd be doing a grievous injustice to my dear wife's memory, if I had had anything to do with a creature like that.'

'Right. Yes, of course. Had to clarify that.'

Jeremy spoke up and asked the Judge, 'Did the man or the woman have any surviving relatives or family members, who would consider avenging their deaths? It seems a bit farfetched, even to me, but someone may have mistakenly considered the double deaths, as gross injustice.'

'No, not to my knowledge. I don't think the couple had any relatives at all, at least none came forward, and their two small children had to go into foster homes, as they had nowhere else to go, after they were orphaned.'

'So there were two children?'

'Yes. There were two boys, if I remember correctly. Or maybe a boy and a girl. I can't be sure. It happened a long time ago.'

'Quite, but can you vaguely remember, how old they were, at the time?'

'No. But I suppose all that information will be available, in the case files, if they haven't gotten blitzed in the war, that is. But I am quite sure, that both children were quite young, definitely below ten, at the time.'

'We'll follow it up. We could find out where those children are now. They must be young adults by now, that is, if they survived the war.'

'Well yes. I didn't think of that. Do you think, that either of them, could have anything to do with...?'

'Not really. It is rather farfetched but at this point in time, we can't overlook any theory, however remote the possibility maybe.'

'Yes, rather. Please keep me posted if you do manage to find out, where they are now. I would like to help them, in any way that I can,' the Judge said in a voice, which carried little or no conviction of his intention to help Lucy Jones' surviving children, and Inspector Thomas found himself thinking, *There seems to be a lot more here, than meets the eye.*

Chapter Nine

Inspector Thomas was agitated as he led the way downhill from Ravenrock House. On a beautiful day like this, the view from the path was spectacular. The river, below, glistened in the Sun, and the knee-high grass bordering the steps, swayed to and fro, in an orchestrated fashion, dancing to the breeze. A few steep steps down, the inspector paused to catch his breath, and said, 'That interview's just opened a can of worms. I had no idea, that the Honourable Judge had such a colourful past. Quite the dark horse.'

Inspector Parker responded, as he caught up with him, 'As dark as they come! But let's give him the benefit of the doubt. It may, in fact, have been an open and shut case, as the Judge claims it was.'

Jeremy spoke up, 'Anyhow, we'd better check up on this old case. It may not seem as cut and dried as the

Judge claims it was. After all – there were double deaths in its wake. Two young children orphaned, on top of that.'

Parker spoke, 'I have an idea, that one of them could possibly have been Mike Murray.'

Thomas responded, 'But he said, that their family name was Jones.'

Jeremy said, 'That doesn't matter. If they were taken into foster homes, and later legally adopted by some other family, it's quite possible, they may have completely different names by now.'

'And that may explain, why Edith was so interested in Mike Murray. Perhaps she did a bit of her own digging, and found out their current whereabouts. The Judge, himself mentioned, what a kind hearted and selfless woman she was. Calling Murray here, might have been her idea of a good deed,' Inspector Parker said, as they resumed walking.

Inspector Thomas, who was right behind Inspector Parker agreed. 'He also mentioned that she had been enthusiastic about something before she died. 'Renewed vigour' he called it,' the inspector said, glancing at his notes from the interview.

'She may have been, under some misguided notion, that she could help them. And if the Judge was guilty, he may have disliked the idea, of facing them, very much,' Jeremy contributed.

'I'd say! But even so, let's assume for a moment, that he finds out his sister has written to one of the children, without consulting him.'

'Yes?'

'So he goes off the bat, and decides to do his sister in? And then his own daughter? And when this chap - Mike Murray arrives, he kills him too? Doesn't sound right somehow,' Thomas said.

Jeremy answered, 'I wouldn't brush this theory off, just yet. Fear can make men do incredibly strange and unnatural things. After all, Edith was killed in the most non violent way possible. I can see the Judge putting an extra sachet of sleeping powders in her milk. And it would also readily explain, why Adelaide refused to divulge the name of the person, she had seen, poisoning her aunt's glass. After all, the child may have been stupid, but I'm sure, she was intelligent enough to know, that her father would hang, if he were convicted of her aunt's murder. And her loyalty for her father, far exceeded the loyalty, she may have felt for her aunt. She couldn't get herself to do it, and was consequently killed for it.'

'But he has a rock solid alibi, for the time the child was drowned. We double checked, just in case.'

Parker responded, 'I agree, that we do need to dig a little deeper, and find out more. He could have had an accomplice. The case is far too murky at the moment, and we may be on the wrong track entirely. It all depends on what we can find out. We need to know more about it. There must be some connection.'

Jeremy said, 'I think, I'll go up to London tomorrow, and catch up with some old friends at Scotland Yard, and see what I can fish out, about this old case. It must have been quite a high profile case, in its time, seeing that the Judge himself, was directly involved.'

'I'm amazed that it didn't create a scandal, what with the young secretary, and the sex angle involved, irrespective of what the outcome was,' Thomas said.

Parker responded, 'That doesn't surprise me. If there wasn't enough hard evidence to prove otherwise, it would have come down to a respectable Judge's word against an ordinary working woman or man's word. Besides, the fact that the man had come armed, and tried to kill the Judge, must have swung the law, in the Judge's favour. To my mind, it sounds incredibly fishy, that the Judge was as innocent, as he claims to be. I think he denied the alleged affair, a tad too hotly, given that it happened two decades ago. And short of calling the young woman a tart, did you notice that he did everything to malign her character, in front of us. What if she wasn't? What if she was just a young, hard working mother, of two young children, and the Judge took a fancy to her?'

'You have a point there. I'm getting the feeling, that he may have done more, than just take a fancy to her,' was Inspector Thomas' response.

'Quite. And as for Jones, drunk or not, no man in his right mind would go about shooting another, let alone, a senior Judge, unless he had very good reason to do so, and was pushed beyond a point of endurance. And a case like this, would definitely be hushed up, to protect the credibility, of not just one Senior Judge, but to preserve the image of the entire Judiciary, which would otherwise be irreparably tarnished,' Parker added.

'I agree. You are quite right, Inspector Parker. In my experience at Scotland Yard too, I've seen bigger cases than this one, get quietly and effectively brushed under the rug, when influential people are involved. Unless the officiating detective is relentless, in the pursuit of truth and justice, it's known to happen - under the misguided notion, of covering up, 'allegedly' for a greater good. Cases like this, are sometimes quickly hushed up, before the fourth estate, even gets a whiff of foul play.'

'And I have a meeting, coming up this Tuesday, in London, with a select group of my friends. We meet from time to time, to discuss current political scenario, business and industry issues, apart from unusual cases of the day. I'll try my darndest to find out, from my circle of friends in the Judiciary, if there's any truth in our conjecture. Someone is bound to have the inside picture on Judge Wilson,' Inspector Parker said by way of explanation to Thomas.

'Inside information is exactly what we need, at this point. Any road, we'll get a much clearer picture, once you dig up the case details, from your Scotland Yard chums, Detective Richards. And er... from your circle as well, Inspector Parker. Talking about dark horses, I wasn't aware, that you are part of British Intelligence.'

'Never mind that, Inspector. I never said, I was, and you never heard it from me.'

'Right! Mum's the word. I think I owe you both, an apology. I am glad that you are here. Before this, I wasn't so sure it was a good idea at all, to have you both down here. I've always held good the theory, about too many cooks and all that. But now, I'm sure we'll get much further, if we put our heads together, on this one.'

'Why, Inspector Thomas, there is no need for an apology... I for one, can completely understand your initial reservations, on finding us nosing about on your watch,' Inspector Parker said kindly.

Jeremy added with a smile, 'And I for one, will have no objection, if you would like to make up, for your default theory around cooks, by sponsoring a round of pints at the pub, at the end of the day.'

'The things I have to put up with, just to solve a case,' he said, shaking his head with mock seriousness and then boomed, his usual exuberance reinstated, 'just having you on... you've got it lads!'

Chapter Ten

The weather at Dartmouth had turned and for the next two days, the Sun had disappeared behind slate grey storm clouds. Monday dawned dark and dreary and the incessant rain, which had fallen steadily through the night, hammering a cacophonic rhythm on the window panes, had brought down the temperature significantly. The howling wind that accompanied it all night long, had also done nothing to aid the inhabitants of Falcon's Crest, in their quest of a good night's rest. Consequently, Sofia awoke feeling rather under the weather. As she wrapped herself in a warm dressing gown, she rang the bell to summon her maid, Marie.

Marie walked in and said, 'Bonjour, Madame. There is a telephone call for you from Ravenrock House. It is Mrs. Belloni. If you would like to take it in the sitting room, I will bring your morning coffee there.'

'Thank you Marie, but I don't feel like having coffee this morning. The very thought is making me nauseous. Can you get me a glass of lukewarm lemon tea instead? Without sugar, of course.'

Marie replied with some disdain, 'Madame, there are no lemons to be found in this country. Is Madame feeling, not so well, this morning? I can prepare a tisane, if Madame so wishes, with rosemary or *verveine.*'

'Oh, I keep forgetting that we're not in America anymore. Verveine will do just fine, thank you Marie. It's just morning sickness, I suppose. I had better go and see what Mrs. Belloni wants.'

Sofia made her way to the sitting room on the ground floor of the house and despite the gloomy weather outside, she felt instantly uplifted. This room was decorated just as she wanted it. This was her sitting room and had been done up in Victorian style. It had a traditional English fireplace and high ceilings. The tall French windows overlooked the extensive lawns dotted with flowerbeds. The soft furnishings were colour coordinated blends of different textured fabrics - beautiful chintz, silk and lace. Soft cushions added to the comfort and grace of the elaborate chintz sofas and Louis XIV armchairs.

The highlight of the room was a miniature antique chandelier made from a thousand tiny droplet crystals - an exquisite affair bought from one of Venice's once-noble-now-impoverished villas. Strategically placed antique Belgian mirrors, gave the room added elegance and reflected her beloved Tissot paintings which captured the iridescent beauty of Kathleen Newton, who was the artist -Jacques James Tissot's lover and muse. At the height of her fame, Sofia had attended a glittering pre-war Tissot art exhibit at London's Leicester Galleries, and had been deeply moved by Kathleen's star-crossed life story. Tissot's life-like paintings had captured her imagination. Her all-time favourite painting, in which Kathleen was depicted reading to her little girl, seated on a bench in the garden, on a sunlit afternoon, gave her a catch in her throat, everytime she saw the scene. To her mind, it captured the essence of pure love, gentle living and the unique bond between mother and daughter. They were given pride of place, on the opposite wall.

She smiled, as she thought how different this room looked, compared with her husband's minimalistic decor, on the top floor, and how strange it was, that two people living under the same roof, could have such diametrically opposite tastes in interiors and still live in perfect harmony. The thought crossed her mind that perhaps, it was because she came from a humble background; she valued beautiful antiques far more than her husband, who had grown up surrounded by them, and hence placed very little value on them.

She walked to the Venetian desk with exquisite gold inlay work and sat on a matching Louis XIV fauteuil. She switched on the beautiful Tiffany stained-glass lamp, which had also been handpicked by her, from an antiquities shop in Paris, along with the exquisitely hand crafted set of silver ink wells and antique desk blotter which were 19th century antiques, dated around 1870s and had supposedly graced the desks of nobility. She looked about her with pleasure. The sight of so many beautiful things, she had bought with love and reverence, with the money she had made from her acting career, gave her a renewed sense of joy, everytime she saw them. And she fervently hoped that she would never live to see the day, she would become blasé to all the beauty that surrounded her, the way a lot of wealthy people, who simply acquire possessions for the sake of it, tend to be. She gingerly lifted the telephone receiver, another favourite possession; made with polished mahogany wood inlaid with ivory flowers, and spoke into it.

'Hello.'

'Hello, Sofia, how are you? I hear congratulations are in order! Dr. Meadows was here, earlier this morning, for father's routine health to-do and gave me the wonderful news. Does Henry know yet? How perfectly exciting, it must be for you!'

'Yes, it is rather exciting, isn't it? To be honest, the news came as quite a relief to me. I had been feeling quite ill and went to Dr. Meadows, for a check up. I was a nervous wreck, I can tell you that. And it came as an enormous relief, when the doctor informed me that I was in the family way and, not dying theatrically from consumption or some such awful thing.'

'Sofia! You can be so funny, but why on earth, would you think that?'

'Well, honey, as they say, back home in Missouri, I ain't no spring chicken, you know!'

'Piffle. You are as young, as you think and look. Why, you could pass off for a twenty five year old, even on one of your bad days! And the news must have made Henry so happy!'

'Oh, I think Henry is yet to recover from the news. Of course, he was the first person I told, but judging from his reaction, and the fact that he took the very next train to London and I haven't heard from him since, I feel that I ought to wait before I inform Helen. If she is her father's daughter, which she is, in spades, God only knows, how she will react!'

'Nonsense! I'm sure Helen will be delighted and Henry probably had some urgent business to attend to in London. Besides, everybody knows that women in this condition are more often than not, prone to strange fancies, so if I were you, I wouldn't read too much into that.'

'Oh, Henry will be fine, I know, but Evelyn, I haven't breathed a word about it to Helen, yet. I'd much rather that she heard the news from Henry – after all, he is her father, and will know best, how to break the news to her. So, hush, my girl and not a word about it to anyone till he gets back from London.'

'Quite right, consider my lips sealed. By the way, the reason I called, apart from conveying my heartfelt congratulations of course, is that I need some help. I want to borrow the girls, Helen and Rachel for a day. The thing is, Sofia, I have the unhappy task of clearing up Adelaide and Aunt Edith's things, from their rooms, and I can't do it alone. The only other woman in the house is the clumsy new parlourmaid and I don't really fancy the idea of her going through and sorting their personal and intimate things. To cut a long story short, I've been putting it off for some time now, but Dr. Meadows seems to think, and rightly so, that doing that might bring some normalcy back to the house and our lives.'

'Yes, I too think, it makes perfect sense. The sooner you do it, the better it will be for everyone. And I am sure the girls will be happy to help you, in any way they can. Rachel's husband, Jeremy left for London this morning. And as it stands, they probably have nothing much to do, in this weather. I'll ring you back and let you know, what time they can join you.'

'You are a darling, Sofia. Tell them, I'll give them a sensible working lunch – probably sandwiches made from fish or crab paste.'

'Ugh, I think, for our plan to work, I had better not mention that,' Sofia said, scrunching up her face, as she heard Evelyn's laughter, on the other end of the line.

'Well then, I must trot along now. And thank you so much. Take care, and goodbye,' Evelyn said, as she rang off.

Chapter Eleven

The steam train from Devon promised to make the journey up to London in six hours. They were half way there, and Jeremy and Inspector Parker moved to the dining car for lunch and discussed the case. The train swerved, just as Jeremy spooned soup, into his mouth. The resulting spill landed on his tie, and made a wet patch on it.

'Blast!' He cursed out loud, as he tugged for his pocket handkerchief, a folded note paper fell out of his coat pocket. He bent down to pick it up and read the first line.

'I say! Take a look at this, Inspector. Seems to me, we are on the right track. This definitely looks like a threatening note.'

Inspector Parker smoothed the note down on the table cloth and read out the type-written content slowly, *'If you value your wife's life, drop this investigation and*

leave Dartmouth. And take the apprentice with you.
If you do not heed this advice, your wife will be next.
Make no mistake. Yours truly - A well wisher.'

Parker exclaimed indignantly, 'Well, I'll be dashed! I
don't know which I find more offensive - the fact that this
chap is threatening to murder your wife or that he refers
to me as a bloody 'apprentice'. I can't wait to get my hands
on him now. But I do think, just to be on the safe side,
we ought to send Miss Rachel, er, I mean Mrs. Richards,
back to Rutherford Hall.'

'Somehow, I don't see that happening. If I know
Rachel, one look at this note and wild horses won't drag
her away from Dartmouth, until we get to the bottom of
this!' Jeremy said, with a slight smile.

'Yes, you have a valid point there. She's as fearless as
they come. But she almost got herself killed the last time
she got involved. I'm not so sure, I want to put her in
danger, a second time.'

'The last time, the murderer took us by surprise. This
time, we'll be better prepared. The first thing we'll do,
once we get to London, is make a telephone call and
inform her and Sofia about this. She'll be on her guard,
and I know Sofia keeps a Colt 32 in the house.'

'I still don't like it. And then there's the question, as
to how on earth this person managed to plant the note
in your pocket? Could someone have slipped it in, at the
station? Do you remember anyone brushing past you?'

'No, my instincts tell me that the murderer is someone
closer to home. I can bet my life on it. All they had to do
was walk up to the coat stand in the hall and slip it in,

anytime, over the past few days. I don't bother to check my coat pockets. For all you know, if I hadn't split the soup, we wouldn't have discovered it, till we got back home to Sunny Ridge! This means, that anyone could have planted it there – anyone at Ravenrock, Falcon's Crest or even at the hospital. Those are the only places where I left my coat unattended, for any length of time.'

II

At three in the afternoon, Jeremy and Inspector Parker parted ways at Waterloo station after making the phone call to duly warn the ladies. They managed to get Sofia on the line, and she informed them that Rachel and Helen had gone across to Ravenrock House a few hours ago. When Jeremy read out the content of the letter, Sofia sounded concerned, and promised him that she would inform Rachel about this new development.

Outside the station, Jeremy hailed a taxicab.

'Where to, guv'nor?' asked the ruddy cheeked taxi driver.

'Scotland Yard, my good man, and make it sharp. There's an extra five shillings in it, if you do,' he instructed the driver. He wanted to get his work done and head back to Dartmouth as soon as possible – by the morning train, if possible. Something about the whole set up at Dartmouth worried him, but he couldn't quite put his finger on what it was, exactly.

The taxicab driver took on the instruction with enthusiasm and almost made Jeremy rue his words, as on every turn, the taxi careened too close for comfort, towards the pavement as it made its breakneck way through London's streets. But the upshot was that they reached Scotland Yard in five minutes flat and Jeremy left the driver, grinning with a large tip.

'If you want, I'll wait for you guv'nor. If you have to go places, you can hire my services and this fine taxi, for the rest of the day.'

'Right, I'll hire your services till tomorrow. I may have to run around London for a bit today. Wait for me here. Just make sure that where ever we go, you must get me back to the station tomorrow morning, in time to catch the first train back to Devon.'

'Yes, Sir! I'll do that, to be certain.'

'What is your name, my good man?'

'It's Duke Wellington, Sir.'

'Really! As in Arthur Wellesley's nom du jour?'

'I had an ambitious mother, Sir. God rest her soul.'

'Well, Duke, she wasn't quite off the mark. Like your namesake, your activities also seem to revolve around a Waterloo, albeit a different one. That said, you had better wait for a bit. I ought to be out, in half an hour, or so.'

'Right you are, Sir. Ha, ha, right you are!'

Jeremy walked in through the familiar entrance of Scotland Yard and was immediately greeted by Chief Inspector Harrow, who was, on his way out.

'Why, Detective Richards, what brings you back to our hallowed halls?'

'Chief Inspector,' Jeremy acknowledged his greeting, by touching his hat and said, 'Just came by to say hello, and pay my respects to you all.'

'Yes, yes, of course, I don't doubt that for a minute,' said the Chief Inspector, with a shrewd twinkle in his eyes, as the two men shook hands. He continued, 'As you can see, I am just on my way out, and in the interest of saving time, for both of us, why don't you tell me which case you are interested in and I'll direct you to whoever's currently in-charge of it.'

Jeremy smiled back and said, 'Touché! Glad to see, you haven't changed at all, and yes, there is a case I'm a tad bit interested in, but I wish it were as simple as that. Thing is, it's a really old case and dates back about two decades and the timeline could be anywhere from the late twenties to the early thirties. But, it involved an attempted murder on a senior Judge, in London, so I'm assuming, we handled it.'

'Quite possible. In that case, you'll probably want to catch up with the 'Gargoyle',' he said referring to the archives in-charge, Tom Bedlow, who earned himself the legendary status of being a walking human encyclopaedia when it came to crime, information regarding criminals and old cases. No one knew how or when he was christened with the affectionate nickname, 'The Gargoyle', but Jeremy remembered that it had something to do, with the fact, that Bedlow had always claimed with distinct pride, that he was in charge of guarding the archives, or as he put it, 'the gates of hell'.

'Yes, as a matter of fact, I was just headed in his direction,' Jeremy said, pointing to the stairs that led to the basement.

'Then, sadly, you are headed in the wrong direction, Detective, because the Gargoyle retired from service about six months ago and was given a magnificent send off from Scotland Yard.'

'I'm sorry, I wasn't aware of that,' Jeremy said, looking chagrined.

'Yes, quite. If anyone would remember a decrepit old case, down to the last details, he certainly would. However, as things stand, you could still visit the archives. I'd be happy to write out a pass for you, Detective, but I must warn you, that the upstart who has taken charge of the archives, is none other than young Roddy Stewart. I sent him there as a fitting punishment, for strutting about, being a pompous pup most of the time. One feels the need, these days, to teach this brash new breed, some humility. And, I'm afraid, he won't be of much help. The fool has gone and changed the Gargoyle's filing system and it's resulted in an unholy mess in the archives. You may have to spend days, if not weeks, wading through masses of files, by yourself, before you find your ancient case.'

'Oh, bollocks!' Jeremy said, now thoroughly disheartened.

'All is not lost, Detective, there may still be a sliver of hope, yet. I suggest, you poke your head into the administrative section and ask Marge if she can provide you with the Gargoyle's new address. I believe he has moved somewhere in the suburbs to grow things, you know, and is probably pottering about with flora and fauna and such, as we speak. Find him, and chances are, you'll get an insight into the case, assuming of course, that it came under Scotland Yard's jurisdiction.'

III

Jeremy found himself seated opposite Marge Harding, in the administrative wing shortly. Everything looked and sounded just the same, the wood panelling, dusty file cabinets, typewriters clacking away as paperwork was compiled on heavy oak desks and seated behind this one, yet another fixture of Scotland Yard - Marge Harding. She was a stern looking spinster, of medium build, with short curly brown hair that was turning grey at the temples, and attractive brown eyes, hidden cleverly, behind her trademark horn rimmed spectacles. She had taken care of the administrative division, at Scotland Yard, for as long back, as he could remember. Anyone, who didn't know, that she was an integral part of Scotland Yard, would have her down pat, as an efficient secretary, in some publisher's office. She exuded efficiency.

Dressed in a sensible, plain, no fuss, brown skirt suit, she addressed Jeremy, 'There, you are, Detective. Bedlow has bought a house in New Malden in Surrey, I believe. Why anyone would sell a perfectly decent flat in London to go and live in one of those ghastly new suburban estates, is beyond me. Anyhow, good luck with finding him. Once you do, tell him, I said, hello. It seems to me, that as soon as people leave here, they seem to forget I exist. Take you, for instance... ' she said, as she handed over a notepaper, with Tom Bedlow's address, scrawled in her flowing handwriting.

'Thank you. I'll be sure to do that, but, Miss Harding, tell me, how do you do it?'

'Do what, exactly?'

'Get more and more beautiful, with the passage of time,' Jeremy said, with a boyish grin, as Marge Harding got up to put the dusty old ledger back in its place. She turned around and peered at him over her horn rimmed glasses.

'Now, now, Detective Richards, I was given to believe, that a lady, of apparently questionable intelligence, has finally made an honest man out of you. Under the circumstances, it would be best, to change your rakish ways and learn to behave yourself, around allegedly beautiful women,' she deadpanned back at him with a bare hint of a smile.

'Rather difficult, but the attempt must be made, I suppose,' he said with a smile he couldn't suppress.

'Life is full of difficulties. I do hope, you plan to introduce me to your wife, soon.'

'Yes, I will bring her here, the next time she comes up to London, I promise. I'm quite certain, she would enjoy a tour of this old haunt, and more specifically, your company, immensely.'

'I look forward to it,' Marge said, with a smile that reached her eyes.

Chapter Twelve

Meanwhile, at Ravenrock, Rachel was in Adelaide's room, folding clothes into neat piles on the dresser, setting them aside for various charitable institutions and orphanages. She picked up an exquisite black and pink lace negligee, and with a puzzled look at Helen, she couldn't help but blurt out, 'A bit modish for a young fourteen year old, don't you think? I'm surprised to find this amongst Adelaide's things.'

Helen looked up from the desk where she was sorting out Adelaide's papers and school books, and said, 'Why, that little rat! That's mine. She must've pinched it from my room. Sofia gave that to me about a year ago. I wondered where it had gone!'

'Hmm, mystery solved. Here you go,' Rachel said, tossing it across to Helen.

Helen caught it and looked at it in dismay. 'She's worn it and torn it, probably trying to squeeze her fat little bottom into it. Oh, give it away.'

'Somehow, I get the feeling that neither the Salvation Army nor the orphanages would encourage their charges to wear something like this. I'll put it aside,' Rachel said, with a smile.

'What a waste of handmade Belgian lace. If Edith were alive we could've asked her to, at least, fashion lace handkerchiefs out of it. '

At that moment Evelyn walked in, with a tray that held three glasses of Vimto, followed by the parlourmaid who was carrying another tray of sandwiches. Evelyn had overheard the last piece of the conversation and asked, 'Fashion lace handkerchiefs out of what?'

Helen spoke with slight embarrassment, 'Oh, it's nothing, really. Just something that belonged to me and wound up among Adelaide's things, that's all. Better to get rid of it.'

Evelyn spoke to the parlourmaid, 'That'll be all, Agnes. I'll call, if I need you later.'

After the parlourmaid left, closing the door behind her, Evelyn turned to Helen and asked, 'So, what is it?'

Helen showed her.

Evelyn's eyebrow went up, 'Did you give her that?'

'No, but it doesn't matter, really.'

'I always knew Adelaide had her faults, but I never imagined she was a thief. I am sorry.'

Rachel spoke up, 'Oh, no, I wouldn't call her that. She was only fourteen – an awkward age for girls to be at, I suppose, and she may have secretly hero worshipped Helen and wanted to keep something pretty and glamorous that belonged to her.'

'Yes, now that you mention it, she did look up to both Helen and Sofia! I suppose she must've been smitten by all the Hollywood glamour that surrounds one, at Falcon's Crest.'

Helen spoke, 'Sofia certainly is glamorous, but you could hardly categorize me with her!'

'By default, my dear. And possibly by association,' Evelyn said with a sad smile.

'Anyhow, I'm glad you brought us sandwiches. I am absolutely famished. And where did you manage to find Vimto? I haven't seen it since the war began!' Rachel exclaimed.

Evelyn smiled and said, 'I found some at the grocers the other day and practically pounced on it. He said, they'd just revived it. What, with all the sugar rationing, it doesn't taste the same but it's still alright. Thought I'd offer it as a treat for all your hard work! That reminds me, I'm almost done sorting out Aunt Edith's things. The Salvation Amy will be pleased. She didn't have much but everything she owned was good quality and honestly, most of her things look as good as new. And I've seen her in them, for years. I must say, she had quite the knack of maintaining her clothes. But her papers, on the other hand, are in such a mess, especially after the police went through them. Two boxes, full of letters, cut-outs from magazines and newspapers, old invitations, knitting patterns and what not. I have no idea what to keep and what to throw out, simply because I'd have to read through them and I just don't have the time.'

'Well, I'm almost done here. I could sort them, for you, if you'd like,' Rachel said, hoping to find something that would shed light on the case, amongst Edith's old papers. Perhaps, something the police may have inadvertently overlooked.

'Oh, would you? That would be so kind. John has asked me to bring some things he needs, to the hospital and I want to get back and help Agnes start dinner, before it gets late,' Evelyn said, gratefully.

II

Rachel emptied the two boxes on the rug in Edith's room and went to work systematically organizing the papers into relevant piles – documents, letters, news and magazine cut-outs, receipts and so on. She concentrated particularly on the newspaper cuttings to begin with, to see if she could find any reference to the old case, Jeremy had spoken about. There was quite a pile of cuttings but most were related to gardening tips, recipes, and showed that Edith had a passion for both gardening and running the house efficiently. No surprises there. The magazine cut-outs were mostly about knitting, dress patterns, descriptive recipes and ikebana flower arrangements. Again, she found nothing of interest there.

Then she started going carefully through letters. Most were correspondence between friends and family during the war years. She found several receipts for small donations made to charitable institutions over the years.

Rachel smiled to herself and thought that Edith had been a 'closet do-gooder'- the kind of person who gives to charities not for any social recognition or gratitude but because it gives them personal pleasure to do so. In that bundle, she found two letters, postmarked Kent and the content was revealing. Evidently Edith had written to the parish asking about Vicar Griffin's whereabouts. She found herself thinking, *Griffin*. That was John's last name. Then the vicar must have been a relation of his, possibly his father. Rachel wondered why Edith had wanted to get in touch with John Griffin's father.

The answering letter had come from a Mrs. Ansell, who had said that he had passed away in 1937 and that he had been a very kind man and was highly regarded in the community. She even went on to say that the Vicar's kindness had been legendary in those parts, owing to the fact that when the local orphanage had shut down due to lack of funding, he had taken in children from the Three Oaks into his own establishment and later arranged to have them sent to good foster homes. It went on to say that, he had been a pillar of their community while he was alive and was fondly remembered by all who knew him.

The next letter from Mrs. Ansell, dated two months after the first, explained that while she did not know anyone connected to the 'Three Oaks' anymore, but she had given the address of a local man who had been a caretaker at the orphanage for a while. It was a London based address with a telephone number of a public house where one could leave a message for him. The name of the caretaker was Samuel Reid.

Rachel kept both letters. The police had not thought them important or relevant to the case at the time of Edith's death. They had probably assumed that her interest in Three Oaks had stemmed from her other charitable works and donations to similar institutions in the past.

A vague idea was forming in her head that Edith may have innocently stumbled upon something that opened up a larger truth, which someone wanted to hide at any cost. A truth that eventually led to her murder. Why did she not consult John directly about his father? Why did she write to the parish unless she suspected something was amiss? Surely, John Griffin could prove his identity. Or had Edith begin to suspect that he was an imposter? But Mike Murray had recognised John as his commanding officer, in front of two witnesses, so John couldn't possibly be an imposter. Besides, the murderer had targeted him as well. But even so, apart from the army connection, what possible connection did Murray have with the Vicar and the Three Oaks?

There was another possibility. Why had Edith been so interested in the Three Oaks Orphanage? Had it rung a bell in her mind? Was that the orphanage that Lucy Jones' children had been sent to, after their little family unit was tragically torn apart, and was destroyed by ensuing circumstances? Rachel was certain that Edith would have contacted Samuel Reid. She also knew from what Jeremy had told her, that Edith had written to Mike Murray and invited him to visit her at Dartmouth. Why? Had she got his name from Samuel Reid? Had Edith finally stumbled upon Lucy Jones' surviving progeny and decided that she wanted to help them. And why was Edith killed even before Mike Murray showed up? Who was Mike Murray really and why was he killed? The key was to find Samuel Reid and ask him what Edith had wanted.

There was so much going on in her head that she wanted to desperately speak to Jeremy, to clear her head and tell him about her find. Perhaps she could compel Jeremy to meet Samuel Reid in person, while he was in London.

She decided to leave a message for Jeremy at his club, to ring her urgently. She knew he would spend the night there, in case he decided to stay back in London. Now, she hoped he would. It would save them a second trip to London. She also decided to ring the public house and leave a message for Samuel Reid.

Chapter Thirteen

Jeremy stepped out of Scotland Yard and stopped by the phone box across the street and made some calls. Something urged him to call Rachel. He placed a call to Falcon's Crest and the maid, who answered the phone, informed him she was still not in, so he left a message for her that she was to wait for his call at eight thirty in the evening. He would be at his club by then. The next call he made was to the Gargoyle's number, which Marge Harding had provided. He hoped that he would be able reach him. Luckily, Tom Bedlow was in and happy to hear his voice. When Jeremy told him that he'd like to visit and gave him a brief idea of what he was after, he could hear the enthusiasm in Bedlow's voice. 'Wilson, yes, Judge Wilson. I do recollect the case but it was so long ago, I'll have to jog my memory for that one. The old grey cells are not what they used to be, Detective.

It will come to me, hopefully by the time you get here. But don't worry, I'll consult some of my old case books from the twenties.'

By then, Duke had spotted Jeremy and driven the taxicab up to the phone box.

'Next stop New Malden, Duke. Do you, by any chance, know your way about the new estates that have sprung up there?' Jeremy asked Duke, as he shut the taxicab's door.

'Aye, guv'nor, don't I just! I have an aunt who lives that way and her family runs a tobacconist's shop on Grafton road. I like that place, decent it is. Most posh people look down on the suburbs and some of them hoity-toity ones are just nasty about it, but I ask you, guv'nor, what's wrong with the working class wanting to get away from dingy London lodgings and owning their own bit of house and garden?'

'I couldn't agree more, Duke. I myself moved away to the country and bought a cottage. There is a singular charm to owning one's own place and as you say, I too feel people who mock the new developments are being a tad unfair. Anyway, it's 'The Crescent', we want.'

'Right, guv'nor,' Duke said, as he steered the taxicab back on to the road.

For the next fifteen minutes, as they drove, Jeremy's mind went silently to some lines Rachel had only recently read out to him. A verse written by the poet Hilaire Belloc, that voiced, in no uncertain terms, what the British upper classes thought the new suburbs represented: *'Miserable sheds of painted tin, Gaunt villas, planted round with stunted trees, And, God! The dreadful things that dwell therein.'* Though he smiled at the humour in the last line, he wondered what the Gargoyle would have to say to someone like Belloc.

What had further surprised him was the fact that, it wasn't just the upper classes but even a regular Londoner like Marge Harding had made it perfectly clear that she despised the new estates. He knew that she lived alone, in a tiny flat within walking distance of Scotland Yard. It made him wonder about human nature and how perceptions differed. In this case, he felt that snobbery could indeed begrudge oneself and others, the golden opportunity to lead a better quality of life. The suburbs weren't as bad as writers and poets of the day, made them out to be. The Government had put protective measures in place and jerry-building days were over. From what he could see, as they drove along, there were detached and semi-detached mock ups of various styles – Tudor, Queen Anne, Georgian, Edwardian, Chalet. Almost all had one thing in common though – bay windows. He had read somewhere, that proud suburban home owners were particular about having bay windows, as that one feature, differentiated their homes from Council houses. He smiled as it occurred to him that snobbery, did in fact, exist at all levels. He was still musing over the irony of things when Duke informed him that they had reached The Crescent.

Jeremy consulted the paper Marge Harding had given him, once again and said, 'We need to look for a place called 'The Laurels'.' They drove for a few hundred yards through the semi-circular avenue, freshly planted with young trees on either side. The homes in the Crescent faced a large oval park. After driving past several differently styled homes with imposing names as 'Mon Repos', 'Arcadia', 'The Wee Nook', 'Grey Gables', they stopped in front of a Swiss Chalet type house that had the desired name board. Jeremy got out of the car and said, 'I won't be long, Duke. This business will probably take about half hour, or so. You could use the time to visit your aunt if you want, as long as you get back in thirty minutes or thereabouts.'

'I'll be back in twenty, guv'nor,' Duke said, giving him a big smile, displaying his uneven tobacco stained teeth.

II

The door was opened by a plump cheerful woman in a peach floral print dress with an apron tied in front.

Jeremy greeted her. 'Good afternoon. I'm Jeremy Richards. I'm here to meet Mr. Bedlow. I believe he is expecting me.'

'Yes, Sir, he informed me you'd be visiting. I'm his housekeeper – Mrs. Hanes. You could take the back way and you'll find him out in the garden.'

Jeremy thanked her and took the narrow pebble strewn path which led him to the back garden. The garden looked picturesque in the mellow afternoon Sun. As he opened the small wooden gate and walked on to the lawn, a Jack Russell terrier rushed up to him, wagging his tail and barking a cheerful greeting. Jeremy bent down, petted him and said, 'Now, who might you be, little fellow?' The Terrier chose to roll over on the grass and expose his belly, and licked Jeremy's hand vigorously, in further appreciation for services rendered in the tummy tickling department. As Jeremy straightened up, the dog jumped up and put his muddy forepaws on his trousers, barking in friendly conversation. In the distance, Tom Bedlow lifted his head up from the flower beds and waved at Jeremy, 'Over here, Detective. And Terry... how many times do I have to tell you, it's not polite to hound unsuspecting guests, like that.'

The terrier cocked his head to one side, gave a cheerful bark and ran towards his master. Tom Bedlow looked a little older than Jeremy remembered. His hair had turned completely white and he was wearing a shabby looking pair of brown gardening trousers and a simple white shirt. He had been busy spraying flower beds. So this, Jeremy thought to himself with a smile, was the life the Gargoyle had finally chosen – surrounded by his flora and fauna, as the Chief Inspector had put it.

They shook hands and sat out in wicker chairs on the lawn and Jeremy looked around appreciatively, and said, 'Nice little place you have here, Tom.'

'It'll do. It's all I can afford, on her Majesty's pension. Besides, it gives me the chance to exercise my green thumb and grow my own potatoes. A lot better than those poky little rooms, I was cooped up in, for the past forty years, I can tell you that! And I have Terry, for company now. It suits us. Oh, but never mind all that, I remembered a few rather interesting bits about your old case,' Bedlow said with a sparkle in his grey eyes.

'Yes?'

'To begin with, it had hush orders. From the powers that be.'

'I thought as much.'

'Not only that, Detective, it was assigned to Judge Greene,' Bedlow said, with meaning in his voice.

'Ah,' Jeremy said, letting the import of his words sink in. Judge Greene was perhaps one of the few Judges in the history of the Judiciary who had been summarily caught and dishonourably discharged, for allowing bribes to sway his judgement.

'Anything else?' Jeremy asked.

'Yes, the young man, Jones was sentenced to life and put away with the criminally insane, in Dartmoor, no less.'

'Oh, God!'

'There's more - his wife's death, shortly after the sentencing was most unfortunate. It was concluded that she committed suicide by jumping on to a railway track and got hit, head-on by the oncoming train.'

'You don't believe that version?'

'I neither believe nor disbelieve. There were two witnesses who testified that she did indeed jump on to the track in an attempt to take her life, and succeeded in doing so...'

'Something tells me, there's more.'

'Well, here's the interesting part. Later, the investigating officer let on, that one of the witnesses had been in the Honourable Judge Wilson's employ, as a footman, a few years prior to the event.'

'Ah! I see.'

At that moment, the cheerful housekeeper who had greeted him at the door brought out a tea tray laden with a teapot and homemade scones, and placed it on the wicker table, in front of them and asked if they'd like anything else. Jeremy thanked her with a smile of appreciation and shook his head at her offer.

Bedlow spoke up, 'May I ask, why the sudden interest in this old ghost of a case?'

'Well, Tom, I can't be sure but it seems to me, that the ghost of this particular case, has come back to haunt the Honourable Judge and the rest of his family,' Jeremy said, and went on to briefly describe the deaths at Dartmouth.

Bedlow heard him out and said, 'Yes, now that you mention it, I did read about two people who had drowned - the young girl and that man but didn't know there was any connection between the two. Also, you say, his son-in-law was almost killed and that sister died under mysterious circumstances too. Very interesting, indeed.'

'Isn't it? Another thing I wanted to ask you about the case - I was also given to believe that the Jones' had two young children. Do you know what happened to them? And did either one, have a name like Michael or Mike?'

'That's right. Two children, I remember them well. I'm quite sure their names were different, though,' he said as he picked up an old weather beaten leather diary with case notes and went through the pages. 'Yes, it says here, their names were Darrel and Robin, aged ten and five respectively, at the time this case was tried. I normally never get emotional over cases, one can't afford to, in our line of work. But I remember feeling rather heartbroken for those little ones, especially after the news of their mother's alleged suicide. I couldn't bear to think about the bleak future that awaited them. Till this day, I sometimes wonder what happened to them.'

'I believe they were sent to some orphanage. Would you, by any chance, know which one?'

Tom Bedlow sighed, 'No, I'm afraid, my case notes end there. It was partly cowardice, on my part. I didn't want to know more. I couldn't deal with the haunted look on their little faces. I saw them walking together, holding each other's hands, ever so tightly, when they were brought in to identify their mother's mangled body.' At this point Jeremy saw a shadow come over Bedlow's eyes, as he continued with his narration. 'The older child identified her. There was no one else to do the job. They had no other family members and by then, their father was in prison, a long way off.'

'What about neighbours, or friends, or even Judge Wilson?' Jeremy asked.

'The couple had already got such negative press. Father convicted for attempted murder, and doing time at dreaded Dartmoor, a depressed, suicidal mother; it didn't surprise me that the neighbours didn't want to get involved. Judge Wilson was out of town when the accident took place. No friends of the family, if they had any, came forward, not even to help the children. I believe, the older child took care of the little one – bathed, dressed and fed his little charge, that sort of thing. You know, I've often wondered, if I could've done something more for them. Anything. But then, what could I have done? A lonely old bachelor like me, I couldn't possibly offer them a home... I barely had one myself. And I had faith in the system, the State. But, whatever excuses I give myself, I do wish, in retrospect that I had done more.'

'You do seem to remember them quite vividly.'

I'll never forget them, the little one, especially. A beautiful child. Seemed small for a five year old, so fragile and helpless. The older one put on a brave face, almost as if he were doing so, for the sake of the little one, but even so, I still remember that lost look in his eyes. They were so quiet. Unlike any other children I had ever seen. Even in their grief, holding each other, silent tears streaming down both their faces. I've never seen two children more alone in this world. There are some sights that stay with you, all your life, even if, those are the very ones, you really want to forget.'

'You're a good man, Tom,' Jeremy said, as he leaned forward and patted the old man's shoulders.

'No, I'm not. Far from it. I can't help but think, that in losing a part of his family, the Judge is finally getting a taste of his own medicine back.'

'Come, now, Tom - you don't really mean that.'

'If I have ever encountered pure evil, Detective Richards, it was in this case. You see, *I know* that the Judge single-handedly and wilfully destroyed four innocent lives and got away with it.'

Chapter Fourteen

Jeremy finally managed to get through to Rachel from his club. She had been waiting for his call. He felt an enormous sense of relief just to hear her voice. Though he had brushed away the threatening letter, something gave him the premonition that Rachel was in very real danger. While it was not just the letter, he couldn't quite put his finger on what had triggered his sixth sense.

Rachel had taken Sofia's permission to take his call in Sofia's Victorian sitting room, where she was sure their conversation would not be overheard. They briefly updated each other about the progress they had individually made. Jeremy promised that he would try and track down Samuel Reid and find out more about 'The Three Oaks', and what Edith had wanted to know, first thing in the morning.

Rachel was still recovering from what Bedlow had told Jeremy. Out loud she said, 'It sounds so unbelievable that anyone should go to such lengths and cause so much harm. What a heartless thing to do to those children. Ugh. It is beyond me. To think, that sweet old man, is in reality, such a monster. And I was in his house today, Jeremy.'

'I know. Be careful, darling. This case is really murky at the moment. People are not what they appear to be, on the surface. I sense that there's a dangerous lunatic about, who is cleverly hiding behind a mask of apparent normalcy.'

'But Jeremy, think! If this Judge Wilson chap is as ruthless as Bedlow claims he is, he just may be our man. If killing people or having them killed seems to come naturally to him. It may not matter to someone as psychotic as him to bump off members of his own family. Especially, if they've uncovered the truth. People like that, can go to any length to save their own hides. He obviously has no conscience. Edith found out and he silenced her. Adelaide saw him putting the powder in Edith's glass and she was the next to go. Mike Murray was probably one of Lucy Jones' children and the Judge had to kill him too.'

'What about John Griffin?'

'I think John is scared. I think he suspects someone or something. Oh, I forgot to tell you. While I was at the hospital, Helen mentioned that you were ex-Scotland Yard and John categorically asked me to inform you that he wants a word with you, in private, about something. What if he knows something and the Judge is trying to bump him off as well?'

'What? When was this? Rachel, this could be important,' Jeremy was almost shouting.

'I'm sorry, I clean forgot. Yesterday, about the same time you went with the Inspector to interview Judge Wilson.'

'Has he been discharged from the hospital yet?'

'No, Jeremy. Though Evelyn did mention that he will be, in a day or two.'

'Now, listen carefully, Rachel. Under no circumstances, is he to return to Ravenrock, after he is discharged from the hospital.'

'Jeremy, you're not making any sense. Ravenrock is his home. Where will he go?'

'Let him stay a few days at Falcon's Crest. They have plenty of room. Speak to Sofia. They are friends. She's an intelligent woman and a great actress. Tell her to manage it somehow, by cooking up some excuse. Make sure that Captain John Griffin comes directly to Falcon's Crest from the hospital, and stays there for a few days. He'll be safe there. It is imperative that he not go back to Ravenrock. I think he's in a great deal of danger, as it is. The murderer underestimated him once, and will probably not make the same mistake a second time. In fact, I think he may just try something drastic, before too long.'

'Can I at least confide in Helen? She might be able to help.'

'I think Sofia will be a better bet. Whatever you do, don't say anything to anyone tonight. Be very careful and keep your door locked tonight. I'll try and get back by tomorrow evening.'

'You are giving me chills up my spine, Jeremy Richards. I think I might just go cuddle up with Helen in her room. I'll feel a lot safer.'

'No! For once in your life, listen to me. Please stay in your room and lock your door. I'm serious.'

'Alright, alright. I'll do as you say. You can stop having a heart attack now.'

'Right, goodnight then, darling. I will see you tomorrow,' Jeremy said and disconnected.

Before she placed the receiver down, she heard another click. Someone had been listening in, on their entire conversation, on an extension, somewhere in the house.

She darted out to the hall to check if the silent eavesdropper was still there near the hall telephone. There was no one about. She knew the other extension was up in Henry Cavendish's sitting room adjacent to the terrace on the top floor. She decided to go up and investigate. She was half way up the stairs, when she saw Sofia coming down.

Sofia greeted her, 'There you are. I was looking for you.'

'Sofia, do you know if anyone is in your husband's sitting room?'

'Yes, of course, the boys are over from Ravenrock. We're all upstairs on the terrace and I was just on my way to ask if you'd like to join us for a postprandial nightcap.'

'Boys?'

'Antonio and Timothy,' she said and leaned forward in a conspiratorial way to add, 'between you and me, I think Timothy is developing quite a 'pash' for Helen. That's what you young people call it nowadays – 'pash,' isn't it?

Rachel laughed. 'Yes, we do, but somehow, I don't think that Helen feels the same way about Timothy. If you ask me, I rather think, she has a pash for the good captain, instead.'

'John?'

'Yes, didn't you notice how she reacted, when she heard that he was almost killed?'

'Really? I didn't think anything of it then, because the news came as quite a shock for all of us. But, you may have something there. I have never seen her so upset over bad news before, and as it turns out, we've had plenty of bad news over the past few weeks.'

'Exactly. I've known Helen since she was a girl and she's one of the most placid people I know. Her reaction to John's accident surprised me no end.'

'My dear Rachel, has anyone ever told you that you are very clever and observant?'

'I wish someone would tell Jeremy that. He seems to think that I'm a birdbrain who can't fend for herself! Oh! That reminds me, did you see anyone using the phone upstairs?' Rachel asked casually.

'Timothy wanted to make a call to Ravenrock to ask Evelyn if she'd like to join our impromptu party but I'm not sure if he actually got around to doing it. I left to go and get you.'

As Rachel and Sofia walked up together, Rachel wondered if it was Timothy who had lifted the receiver and overheard her conversation. She needed to know.

They joined the others on the terrace and Rachel asked Timothy point blank, 'Is Evelyn going to join us?'

'I don't know, is she?' he replied, reddening.

'Sofia just said you were planning to telephone her,' Rachel said sweetly.

'Oh, I forgot to do that. I was busy having my heart broken, by your dear friend, Helen.'

'Where is she?'

'She went to powder her nose. She's been gone for quite some time... Ah, there she is!' he replied, as Helen rejoined them, holding a glass of red wine.

Rachel turned to tease Helen, 'I've been getting reports, young lady, that you are responsible for this good man's broken heart.'

Helen blushed and then replied, rolling her eyes, 'Nothing of the kind. Timothy takes me aside and proposes to me at least twice a week, out of sheer force of habit and I have to keep saying no, just so he can keep on proposing. It's fast becoming his favourite pastime, and the day I say 'yes', he will probably hate me for it!'

'Just try me!' Timothy said to her.

At that point, Antonio joined them and smiled at Rachel. 'Ah, Bella, it's good to see you. Can I get you some red wine?'

'Likewise, Antonio, it's nice to see you again and I'd prefer white, thank you. Will your wife be joining us?' Rachel asked him sweetly.

'That depends. Will your husband be joining us?' Antonio responded without batting an eyelash.

'I'm afraid, not. He had to go up to London, on work. I'm already missing him, a lot,' Rachel said, with emphasis on the last part.

'Such a pity, but I make sure you don't miss him too much. I'll be back with your wine, Bella. Stay here,' Antonio said, laying on his powerful charm. And then as an afterthought, he turned to Sofia and asked, 'And you Sofia, can I get you something?

Sofia replied, 'I'll come with you and fix myself a Martini. You boys haven't quite got the hang of making one. The last one was much too dry. Come along Timothy, I'll show you both how to get it right.'

As the three of them went out of sight, Helen was giggling. She took Rachel aside and mocked sotto voce, with a thick Italian accent, 'Ah, Bella, you made a conquest. You kill me with your English rose beauty. I drive you in my car into sunset... Ouch!' she said, as Rachel pinched her arm.

'I'd rather drive into a ditch on my own, thank you! For God's sake, keep him away from me,' Rachel grumbled.

'But, why Bella, oh, why?' Helen asked with mock anguish.

'Oh, shut up and behave! I'm married, and blissfully so. And that brings me to something else - why are you turning Timothy down? He seems really nice.'

'I can't marry him. He's just a boy!'

'And you'd prefer someone older, perhaps someone like Captain John Griffin, eh?'

It was Helen's turn to grumble. 'Oh, keep quiet and drink your wine, Bella,' she hissed into Rachel's ears, as Antonio returned holding two wine glasses and a dazzling smile.

Despite her initial reservations around Antonio's overt attentions, Rachel found that she enjoyed the evening immensely. There was a sense of camaraderie among those present and Sofia was a sparkling hostess. Helen put some new records on the gramophone and they laughed, drank and danced under the stars till midnight. Aside from his flirtatious ways, Antonio turned out to be a fantastic dancer and Rachel enjoyed Timothy's dry sense of humour. They were all so tipsy by the end of the evening that Sofia refused to let the boys walk all the way back to Ravenrock and bundled them off to the extra guestroom.

II

It must have been around two in the morning. The house was quiet and Rachel was in a dreamless, wine induced sleep. There was a strange metallic sound coming from the door. Rachel got up with a start.

The room was partially visible as moonlight streamed in through the windows, but the door was in complete darkness. The sound came again.

Rachel froze. Someone was trying her door knob.

She put on her bedside lamp and said out loud, 'Who's there?'

There was no response.

She was tempted to jump out of her bed and open the door to confront whoever was on the other side but then she remembered her tryst with the ruthless murderer at Rutherford Hall and she was not keen to relive that experience. She had not heeded Jeremy's warning the last time and had nearly paid for it with her life.

This time around, good sense prevailed. She got out of bed and armed herself with a poker from the fireplace and dragged an arm chair under the door knob, so that even if the killer managed to force the door open, using a master key, she would not be caught unawares.

There was no further sound and all had gone deathly quiet again, so quiet that she almost thought she had imagined the whole episode. She found it difficult to go back to sleep. But after keeping an hour long vigil, she realised that whoever had made the attempt to open her door, was not coming back.

Keeping the poker by her bedside, she drifted off into a troubled sleep.

Chapter Fifteen

The next morning, Jeremy had breakfasted at the Club and while he waited for Duke to arrive, he placed a call to Falcon's Crest. Rachel informed him about her night of vigil. She conveyed her fears that their conversation was overheard, the night before and related the ensuing unsuccessful attempt, by an unknown assailant, to enter her room. Jeremy instantly made up his mind to take the first train back to her. Samuel Reid could wait. Ten minutes later, the concierge informed him that his taxicab had arrived. Jeremy thanked him and left.

Duke greeted Jeremy as he picked up his bag, 'Mornin', guv'nor. Shall we head to the station, then?

'Yes, Duke, back to Waterloo,' Jeremy said, as he sat in the cab.

As Duke began to drive, Jeremy weighed the situation at hand and spoke, 'Duke, would you be interested in picking up a special commission? I have a job for you. But, only if you are upto it. It involves some amount of detecting and there may be some danger involved.'

'Fire away, guv'nor.'

'It's like this. I need you to locate a pub called 'Ye Olde Goose' somewhere in Lambeth. Here is the telephone number. There's a regular there – goes by the name of Samuel Reid. I need you to locate him and get some information from him and report back to me. This is the number in Dartmouth, where I can be reached.'

'Why is he dangerous, guv'nor? What's he done?'

'It's more about what he knows, Duke. He's not dangerous although he may be in some danger himself. He's one of our main leads at the moment, in this case we're trying to solve. It's imperative that you don't scare him off. He's an old man and used to be the caretaker at an orphanage somewhere in Kent, called 'The Three Oaks'. The information, I need concerns two children in particular – Darrell and Robin Jones, who were sent to the said orphanage about twenty years ago. I need to know what happened to them, after it shut down. And in case they were sent to foster homes or adopted by some family, it will be an added bonus if you can wheedle out the names of the adoptive parents from him. Also, try and find out if he knew the man who recently drowned at Dartmouth; a chap by the name of Mike Murray.'

'I'll do my best, guv'nor but if he's an old timer, he may not remember much. Or worse, clam up on me.'

'You'd be surprised at how much these old timers can recall, if they want to! Look, I have to return to Dartmouth urgently but here's a fiver, buy him lunch and a couple of pints. It may help you befriend him, if he's suspicious at first. And there's twenty quid in it for you, if you succeed.'

'Holy moley, guv'nor! That's a princely sum. I'll do it!'

II

Rachel had cornered Sofia first thing in the morning and explained to her, what Jeremy had requested her to do, in lieu of ensuring that there were no immediate or further attempts on John Griffin's life. Sofia understood and told her that she would do her best to convince the Judge that bringing John to stay at Falcon's Crest was the best possible course of action, without causing undue alarm.

Within an hour after her conversation Sofia was seated opposite Judge Wilson, in his study, at Ravenrock. She had driven the boys back after breakfast and was now at her charming best.

'Really, Judge Wilson, it will be our pleasure to take care of John for a few weeks. I know how difficult the past few weeks have been for you and I thought this would take a burden off.'

'It's very kind of you to suggest it, Sofia, but really, we can't possibly...'

Evelyn, who was also present, spoke up, 'Oh, daddy, it does make sense to let John stay with them till he recovers. We are just so short handed at the moment, with Agnes doubling up as the cook and maid. And John will need help – regular sponge baths, highly nutritive healthy meals and all that. I'm afraid, Agnes will give notice, if I give her additional work.'

'But, my dear...'

Sofia spoke up, 'No more buts, Judge Wilson. It's all settled. We have plenty of staff and John will be taken care of beautifully. Now, don't you worry about a thing. Besides, we are practically a stone's throw away from you and you can visit, as often as you like.'

The Judge realised he was out manoeuvred and acquiesced. 'Well, if you both insist it's a good idea, there's nothing more to be said. I am very grateful for your help, Sofia.'

'Please don't mention it,' Sofia told him with a sweet smile. She couldn't wait to go back and give Rachel the good news.

III

Meanwhile Rachel and Helen were in the sculpting shed. Rachel was taking a look at some of the canvasses against the wall. There was a lot of variety but strangely they gave one a feeling of gloom and depression. They were all dark and disturbing. The portraits had twisted faces, the landscapes were desolate and even the still life depictions of fruits and flowers had a sense of decay about them. One scene in particular caught her attention.

'These are rather good,' she said to Helen, who was moulding a head out of clay on her sculpting table.

'Oh, they are rubbish.'

'No, really, I like the one of the young girl walking on the beach, in the storm, holding on to her hat. It's dark but it's also breezy and nice.'

'Oh, that one is quite nice, actually. The rest are rubbish.'

'Stop being so harsh on yourself. You've always been a great one to put yourself down, Helen. It's time, you realised how much artistic talent you have.'

'I know I have artistic talent, just not as a painter. I do like my sculptures, though. Let me show you what I did two months ago.'

She wiped the clay off her hands on a rag, moved to the shelf in the far corner and took the cloth off one of her sculptures. It was two feet high. As Rachel moved closer to examine it, she gasped, 'Oh, this is so beautiful!' The sculpture depicted a young bathing beauty seated on a rock, immersed in a book. One of her arms was raised to her head as if she was trying to keep her windswept hair out of her face and eyes. The eyes conveyed her rapt attention in what she was reading, even as the wind blew her hair helter skelter. It seemed alive.

'You really need to exhibit your work, Helen. This is truly magnificent.'

Helen answered, as Rachel continued to gaze at its intricate detailing, 'Daddy has promised to arrange an exhibit at the end of next year, provided I have at least twenty five good pieces to exhibit. He has a friend who owns a few art galleries in London. I hope you'll be able to attend.'

'I wouldn't miss it for the world! I'd probably be the proudest person in the room, next to your father of course!'

'I just wish my mother were alive. I do miss her. I mean, Sofia is really nice but she's more of a friend, you know.'

'Yes, I know what you mean. No one can take the place of one's mother. And I do remember your mother. She was so elegant and beautiful,' Rachel said, as she remembered Helen's mother - Theodora Cavendish, in her beautiful flowing dresses and the soft fragrance that seemed to surround her, wherever she went. Rachel had met her on several occasions, when Helen and she were at school together.

Helen covered the sculpture with cloth. 'She was an angel. I felt so lost after she died. No one could ever take her place, ever! And I used to feel that nothing I did would amount to anything or be worth anything, without her. If I had one wish, it would be to turn back time. But one simply can't turn back time, can one?' Helen said, her voice choked with emotion.

'No,' Rachel said simply, as she held her closest childhood friend, to her bosom.

'And hence, all the old paintings you see are not art but my way of finding peace with all that was snatched away from me in life.'

'And have you found it?'

'Not yet but I will. I promise you. I will make my peace soon.'

'I couldn't be happier for you. At least you have clarity now. I know only good can come from that.'

'Yes and it's beginning to show in my work. I am happier now than I have been in a long time. That sculpture is just the beginning,' Helen said with shining eyes.

Chapter Sixteen

A t four in the afternoon, Rachel ran down the steps to greet Jeremy and he embraced her. She held on to him as he ruffled her hair and said, 'Thank God, you're safe, darling. I came back as soon as I could.'

She narrowed her eyes at him and said, 'Don't you ever go off again, leaving me behind like that. I was scared to death last night.'

'I promise, next time we go together. Besides, I promised Marge Harding I'll bring you along next time I visit the Yard.'

'You were gone for a day and you've already made promises to strange women?'

Jeremy smiled and said, 'You needn't worry, darling. She asked me to change my 'rakish' ways.'

Rachel rolled her eyes and as they walked into the house hand-in-hand, she informed him that Sofia and Helen had driven out to bring John Griffin back to Falcon's Crest. And that Sofia was throwing a little dinner party because Henry Cavendish was expected back some time in the evening.

Jeremy responded, 'The poor man. I feel sorry for him already. The man of the house returns hoping for some peace and quiet at home, only to find a houseful of murder suspects, mayhem and strange house guests.'

II

Jeremy and Rachel crossed over on the ferry and walked to the police station. There were several developments since their last visit and Jeremy felt he was duty bound to keep Inspector Thomas updated.

They were immediately shown into Inspector Thomas' room. He was going through some paperwork as they entered. He looked up and waved them in, 'Good evening, Detective, Ma'am, please take a seat.'

Rachel noticed that he was wearing reading glasses and now as they sat, he removed them and sighed, 'I had a strongly worded memo from the Superintendent of Police, asking me to send a report about our progress in the case. It seems that the Judge has written to him, voicing his opinion in no uncertain terms, about the deterioration of investigating abilities and in general, the sluggish way the police force functions around these parts.'

Jeremy responded, 'That sounds familiar, Inspector. Back at the Yard, we faced a fair amount of flak too.

The public expects us to make arrests in record time, preferably overnight. But people in the know, are aware of the consequences of making a wrong arrest and that usually gets far more mud on our faces than anything else. So, I wouldn't worry too much about it, especially after what we've uncovered. And although it may be premature to think that it could be included in the progress report just yet, given that hearsay is inadmissible in court, there is a distinct light visible at the end of the tunnel.'

'I hope you're right, Detective. At the moment it seems like the tunnel is about to cave in, before I can get to it. I've heard rumours of a possible transfer in my duties. Coincidentally, I was up for a promotion this year and I'm afraid, if we don't get to the bottom of this soon, the chances of it coming through will be about as likely, as snow in the Sahara. Dratted case!'

'But Inspector, we have very good news! Jeremy found a threatening letter asking us to leave Dartmouth, and someone tried to enter my room last night, possibly with the intention to murder me in my sleep...'

'And that is good news, because...' asked the puzzled inspector.

'Don't you see? Our line of investigation has the killer seriously worried. We must be on the right track. It has everything to do with the facts we've uncovered about the Judge's old case. Jeremy, tell him,' Rachel prodded him.

Jeremy did. He gave him a detailed account of his interview with Bedlow and the latter's conviction that the Judge had been completely ruthless and ingenious in covering up his crime against Lucy Jones, by eliminating her family, and by default, any further evidence of his crime. He also informed him about Rachel's discovery of Edith's letters, Vicar Griffin's connection to the Three Oaks orphanage and finally the commission to locate and get more information about Lucy Jones' other child and Mike Murray, from Samuel Reid.

By the time he finished, the Inspector had regained his jaunty look. He said, 'I say, that narrows down our suspect list considerably. The Judge being in the primary position. No wonder he's getting antsy and writing letters about the place. He's managed to get rid of one – that Mike Murray chap and now he's probably looking to eliminate Lucy Jones' other child as well. I can't wait to get my cuffs on the bloody bugger.'

'But, Inspector, I very much doubt, it was the Judge who tried my door last night. It must've been someone, from within the household,' Rachel said.

Jeremy interjected, 'Or possibly someone acting on his behalf. You did mention that his son - Timothy, stayed the night.'

'Yes, but...' Rachel answered, unsure of Timothy's involvement. She couldn't bring herself to believe that the affable young man would be capable of such a thing. But, if her experience at Rutherford Hall had taught her anything, it was that murderers were just like everyone else - indistinguishable from normal people. And that, anyone could turn out to be one.

The inspector guffawed, 'There you are! And that reminds me, I don't think it will help the case any further, if people start getting murdered in their beds. I think we'll place a constable guard in the house. We are rather shorthanded ever since the war, but I can probably spare Constable Goole on night watch.'

Rachel blurted out, 'With all due respect, Inspector, I can't say that inspires me with a great deal of confidence.'

'Ma'am, while I agree that Constable Goole is no Sherlock Holmes, he is conscientious and the very presence of a police constable in the house is likely to deter anyone from lurking about, outside people's doors.'

Jeremy nodded, 'I couldn't agree more.'

III

Helen was busy fluffing pillows behind John's back and making sure that he was comfortable.

John grumbled, 'If you are going to make such a fuss, I'd rather you get me some good books to read.'

'Books can wait. Let me get you something to eat first.'

'Stop babying me, Helen. I'm going to get very fat and porky if you continue to treat me like a pet project.'

Helen laughed.

John looked at her as if he was seeing her for the first time. It struck him that she had grown into a very graceful young lady. She had been all skin and bones earlier – a mass of loose limbs, messy hair and enormous eyes. Now, she was just a pleasure to look at. She had put some weight on those bones and under Sofia's expert tutelage, she had turned out perfectly coiffed and elegantly dressed. He noticed that she had started applying subtle makeup. It suited her and brought out her best features.

She had turned into what most men would consider as a certifiable 'sight for sore eyes'.

'What?' She asked with a puzzled look at his face.

'Nothing. I was just looking at you,' he answered with a smile.

'Why?'

'Because truth be told, you seem to have grown up overnight. Where is the girl who used to run about on sticks for legs?'

'Really? That's how you compliment a girl? Captain John Griffin – you seriously need lessons on how to charm women, otherwise you'll stay a bachelor for the rest of your life!' As soon as she said it, she knew it was the wrong thing to have said.

'I am not a bachelor, Helen – I am a widower and a father of a very beautiful girl who used to look very much like you. And I don't really care if I never have any other woman in my life again.'

'I'm so sorry John, you know I didn't mean for it to come out that way. And I do wish you happiness in life again. Perhaps someday you will meet someone and fall in love again.'

'Pamela was one in a million, Helen. She was beautiful, warm, witty, loving and smart - everything I wanted in a wife and she had all the qualities I wanted to see in the mother of my child. Fact is, she very much reminded me of mother and I can't imagine anyone else taking her place.'

'Time, John, give it some time. You ought to know better than anybody else that time has the power to heal anything. Just give it time. Trust me, you will love again someday. A man as gentle and loving as you deserves nothing less.'

'I wish I could believe that. Do you? Or are there things in your life too that are beyond the healing powers of time.'

Helen looked at him contemplatively for a few minutes. Finally she spoke slowly, 'I think we all stumble along in life and find our own way of healing. Sometimes, when it doesn't come naturally, it has to be bent to one's will. One has to do certain things, even if it goes against what you would normally tend to do, just so you can heal.'

'Such as...?'

'Well, in your case I would suggest that you stop being so pig headed about living in the past. And while you're at it, don't wait too long or life may just pass you by. And you will end up existing in only in your past without really ever finding a way to live in the present and walk into the future.'

'My God! I'm impressed. You can hold your own in any argument. You really are all grown up now.'

'I'm glad you noticed. I'm twenty four, John. It had to happen someday! Now, I'm going to go and get something nutritious for you, so your bones snap right back into place in record time,' She said, giving him an indulgent smile before leaving the room.

Chapter Seventeen

Henry Cavendish let himself in with his key and walked into the hall. He took off his suit jacket and dropped his bag onto the parquet floor. He was a handsome man yet there was a look of dejection about him. He seemed to be carrying a great weight on his mind.

He was relieved to find that there was no one about. He walked straight to the tray on the hall table, where his mail awaited him and sorted through the envelopes. He finally found the one he was searching for and took it with him into the library.

Luckily there was no one there either. He needed to be alone as he read it. The sky was overcast and the room was in darkness. He walked to the study table and switched on the Tiffany lamp. His entire future course of action depended on what the letter contained. It was from a medical laboratory in Switzerland. He picked up his pen knife and carefully slit open the fly of the envelope.

As he unfolded the paper and read the words, his face changed. A smile started at the corners of his mouth and finally found its way to the rest of his face in jubilation. All was well. His fears had been completely unfounded. He felt like a carefree young boy who had just got renewed lease on life. The anxiety that had been hounding him and giving him sleepless nights for the past few weeks had just vanished into thin air as if it had been made from pixie dust in the first place. Now, he could share his joy with all those around him.

As he got up from the chair, there was spring in his heart and a song on his lips. He went looking for Sofia.

'Sofia! Sofia! Darling, I'm home!' he bellowed.

Sofia was on her settee in her boudoir, taking a nap. She had been wracked by morning sickness through the better part of the day and was exhausted after the trip to the hospital to bring John Griffin home. She also knew that her exhaustion was partly mental because of the nervousness caused by Henry's impending return. He had been so disconnected from her for the past two weeks that she did know what to expect on his return. Now hearing her husband's voice she quickly got up and looked at the clock. He had come back hours earlier than expected and she nervously ran a brush through her hair, pinched her cheeks to bring some colour into them and smoothed down the wrinkles on her dress before she went out on to the landing. The moment he saw her, he gave her a big smile and ran up the steps two at a time. He had the look of a young virile man. As he reached his surprised wife, he took her in his arms and gave her a long, deep kiss.

She struggled to get out of his embrace and held him by his shoulders and exclaimed, 'Whoa, Henry! What's got into you?'

'What do you mean, what's got into me? Can't a man be happy to see his beautiful wife?'

'A wife, who he has completely ignored for two straight weeks?'

'I'm sorry, darling. I really am. I've been a cad and an utter fool and I'd like to make it up to you. Please let me.'

'You have a lot of explaining to do, Mister.'

'I promise, I'll explain everything to you but right now all I want to do is make love to you first.'

'But Henry! The baby!'

'Oh, hush, the baby won't know a thing. Chap's probably busy minding his own business, if he's anything like me.'

'How can you be so sure it's not a girl?' She asked, in a teasing voice. She was so relieved to see him back as his normal self.

'Because I've already got too many girls in my life. This one is definitely a boy but I do hope he doesn't get my nose.'

'And why not? I happen to like your nose,' Sofia said softly, as she ran a finger over his big beaked nose.

'And I happen to like every inch of you and now let's not waste any more time...' He said, as he held her hand and led her to her bedroom.

II

After leaving John's room, which was a guest room on the recently added wing on the ground floor, near the back garden, Helen was headed for the pantry. As she crossed the hall, she met Jeremy and Rachel as they returned from their visit to the Police Station.

She greeted them. 'Oh, hello, where have you two been?'

Rachel said, 'Jeremy wanted to meet the Inspector and I just tagged along with him to the police station. I wanted some fresh air. Did you manage to bring the patient home?'

'Yes and I've just got him settled in and now I'm going to go and fix him a healthy snack. Carrots, I think! And some cheese and crackers.'

'What a regular little Florence Nightingale, you are! Just make sure you don't feed him too much. Your father's 'welcome home' dinner party starts in two hours.'

'Very funny – John just finished giving me a lecture on somewhat the same lines. Overfeeding, my foot!'

Rachel laughed and asked, 'Is your Dad back yet?'

'No, he's expected back on the 7:28 from London. He ought to be home, just in time to enjoy his party,' she said, grinning and then added, 'Oh, and Rachel, John wanted something to read. Could you do me a favour, nip into the library and pick out a few books for him? We've settled him into the guest room at the back – you remember, the one we took the short cut through, to reach the back garden and my sculpting shed?'

'Of course. I'll do it right now. It'll give Jeremy and me, a chance to say hello to him before the party. Did he ask for any author in particular?'

'No, but I know he loves Charles Dickens and Winnie the Pooh,' she said with a grin.

'Right!' Rachel replied with a smile.

III

Jeremy and Rachel entered the library. It had a musty smell of old leather and stale tobacco. Rachel wrinkled up her nose and said, 'It's so stuffy in here. I'm going to open a window.'

As she went behind the desk and opened the window, a breeze blew in and blew some papers off the desk. Jeremy spoke up, 'Rachel, the papers.'

'Oops. Let me just get a paperweight on those,' she said as she bent down to pick them up, smoothed them and put them back on the desk. The one on top caught her attention. It was the same letter that Henry Cavendish had read half an hour ago.

'I say, Jeremy, take a look at this. What on earth does it mean?'

'Rachel, it's not polite to snoop and read other people's private correspondence.'

'Politeness be damned, and I'm not snooping, just playing detective and you should be too if you want to get to the bottom of this case. I'm serious, Jeremy, you really need to see this.'

Jeremy said, 'Oh, alright. I suppose all's fair in murder and mayhem,' as he came up behind her and looked over her shoulder and read the content. His eyebrows went up. A moment later, he said, 'I really don't think someone's private health issues have anything to do with this case. Besides, all this says, in so many words, is that he has just been given a clean bill of health.'

But Rachel's eyes had taken on a strange faraway look. Suddenly a very disturbing thought flashed across her mind and she was left shaken. She found herself thinking, *'No, it just can't be... But, what if it is?'*

Jeremy asked, 'Why, what's the matter, darling? Did I miss something?'

Rachel came back to the present. She looked a little perturbed but she needed time to think. She didn't want to tell Jeremy what had crossed her mind until she made sure that the thought that had entered her head was not a figment of an overactive imagination. Out loud she said, 'No, you are right. It's none of our business. I'll just put it back.'

After she had put a paperweight on the documents, she changed the subject and said, 'It's time to hunt for Dickens. You look in those bookshelves over there and I'll go through these.'

Five minutes later, Rachel had a copy of 'The Pickwick Papers' and A.A. Milne's masterpiece, 'The House at Pooh Corner,' tucked under her arm and they made their way to meet John.

Chapter Eighteen

John greeted them with a smile as Rachel made per functionary introductions and set the books down by John's side.

'The pleasure's all mine, Detective,' John said, as he held out his hand and tried to get up.

'Please, don't get up, Captain. Did they not advise you complete bed rest?' Jeremy asked.

'Oh, no. In fact they told me at the time of discharge that I need to get strength back in my limbs and I must walk or hobble about, for a bit every day, so that my muscles aren't completed useless by the time my bones heal!' He said, rolling his eyes.

Rachel spoke up, 'Oh, you poor dear, you must still be in a lot of pain though.'

'Not if I don't put any weight on it. Truth be told, ever since they put on this great big whacking plaster cast I can't feel my leg much at all, except for when it begins to itch. Then it's awful. But Sofia has promised to supply me with some knitting needles to scratch the itch, so to speak. And the doctor has kindly given me a fair supply of veronal to help me sleep at night.'

They made some further polite conversation about his injury and John informed them that he could hobble about using his sticks and that to all intents and purposes, he was fairly mobile.

Jeremy ventured to ask, 'By the way, Rachel gave me to believe that you wanted to discuss something in private with me?'

'Did I? Oh, yes. At the hospital. It's nothing really. It was soon after the accident and I was brooding over too many things. I daresay, I tend to over-think things sometimes.'

'Still, it would interest me to know what it was.'

'Well, alright but the reason no longer exists since Sofia has very kindly offered to put me up. Fact is, I didn't fancy going back to Ravenrock for a bit. I had a strange feeling that I'd be doomed, if I had to go back there. Don't ask me why – there is no logical explanation for it, which is why I now think in retrospect that it must have been a touch of nerves so soon after the accident, that's all.'

Rachel gave a quick surprised look at Jeremy who smiled and said, 'I thought as much.'

II

By eight o'clock, the guests had started arriving. Dr. Meadows was the first to be shown into Sofia's sitting room. Sofia looked radiant in a champagne colored gown with Henry by her side as she greeted the doctor. Helen complimented her father as she walked in. 'You look rather dapper tonight, Daddy' she whispered in his ear, admiring his dinner jacket. He smiled at her and said, 'You don't look so bad yourself, my dear.' She was in a sea green gown which highlighted her blue eyes and blonde hair. 'Why, thank you!' she said with a smile and a mock curtsey, as she made her way towards John Griffin, who was on a lounge chair with a footstool to support his leg, across the room. Then Rachel and Jeremy walked in and greeted the others. Rachel looked stunning in an emerald green gown and Sofia showered her with compliments as Jeremy shook hands with Henry Cavendish. Shortly, after that the party from Ravenrock arrived. Antonio, Evelyn, Timothy and Judge Wilson were shown in just as cocktails were being passed around. Evelyn walked up to John and made herself comfortable in a chair by his side as Antonio made his way to where Rachel stood. The Judge joined Henry Cavendish and Jeremy as they discussed the new bill that had recently been passed by the House of Commons. There was a certain bonhomie in the air as subdued laughter and cheerful voices mixed with the tinkling of glasses.

Dinner was announced at nine and they all moved to the formal dining area. The table was set beautifully with crystal and the room was lit with three large candelabras that cast a golden spell on all present. It was a delicious meal despite the rampant food rationing; the French chef,

Andre had managed to rustle up three courses. Cream of parsnip soup was served followed by Boeuf Bourguignon with a side of Lord Woolton pie and the final flourish was a perfectly golden crusted Apple Crumble for dessert.

Just before the coffee was served, Henry Cavendish tinkled his wine glass to get everyone's attention. 'I have an announcement to make. My dear friends, in less than seven months from now, we will have the pleasure of welcoming a new addition to the Cavendish family! Please join me in a toast to my beautiful wife, Sofia, who has made me the happiest man alive.'

'Hear, hear,' Helen cheered as everyone else joined in.

'To Sofia,'

'To the Cavendishes'

'Per il piccolo!'

'Congratulations!'

As Sofia blushed and accepted everyone's felicitations, Rachel was observing one face in particular at the dinner table. It told her all she needed to know. In that instant, she knew that her instincts had been correct and that her fears were well founded. As the killer suddenly locked eyes with her, she felt a chill go up her spine. She knew that she had no proof but her instincts were right. She also knew she was up against a Machiavellian mind, the likes of which she had never encountered before.

In a matter of moments she had gone from feeling satiated after a good dinner to feeling quite sick. She felt helpless. She finally knew who the killer was but she could do nothing about it, for now. She couldn't possibly confide in Jeremy or go to the police until she herself had some evidence to base her theory on. Besides, at this point it was just a hunch - a very strong hunch but nevertheless, one simply couldn't go about accusing someone openly of having committed multiple murders based on a hunch. And there was a possibility that her surmise was wrong and she couldn't possibly confide her fears in anyone until she had established the truth for herself.

As the ladies rose from the table to leave the men to their port and cigars, she could feel the killer's unflinching gaze on her. She tried to catch Jeremy's eye at the other end of the table before she left the room but he was leaning towards Evelyn and saying something. Evelyn nodded at him, as she suppressed a yawn and got up to join the ladies.

The realisation hit her that she would have to be careful and watch her own step from this moment forth. But to her mind, knowing one's opponent was the first step to fighting any battle with courage and Rachel was game. With or without anyone's help, she would do her best to prevent any more lives from being lost, starting with her own. She paused to smile at the killer before she left the room.

Helen took her arm as they walked back to Sofia's sitting room. 'What's the matter with you? You look positively green around the gills!'

'Well, I am wearing a green dress...'

'I'm serious. I think you had better go and lie down. You're probably coming down with something.'

'What, one patient isn't enough for you, Miss Nightingale?'

Evelyn stifled another yawn and spoke up, 'I can't speak for Rachel, but if I don't go home immediately, someone will have to carry me home. And I'm sure the men will take ages over their port and cigars. If you don't mind, I think I'll just drive home.'

Sofia spoke, 'Of course, we don't mind, Honey! Are you sure you want to drive back alone? I could ask Marie to accompany you.'

'Oh, no thank you. It's just ten minutes away and I could drive myself back home, from here, blindfolded,' she said stifling yet another yawn. 'Don't know what's the matter with me! Haven't felt this sleepy in ages!'

Rachel was worried. 'It looks like it's starting to drizzle. The roads may turn slippery. I think we ought to ask Antonio to drive you home.'

'I don't want to bother him. Besides, Antonio gets all sulky if I pull him away from a party. Only trouble is, if I take daddy's car, Henry will probably have to drive daddy and the boys home.'

'I'm quite sure, Henry wouldn't mind that one bit.'

'In that case, please inform daddy and Antonio that I've taken the car home.'

'Right, I'll do that as soon as they join us here,' Sofia assured her.

'Thank you for a lovely evening, and congratulations once more, Sofia. Take care and goodnight,' Evelyn said as she kissed Sofia on both cheeks and bid the girls goodbye.

After seeing Evelyn off, Sofia rejoined them and asked, 'Anyone up for a round of cards, gin rummy perhaps?'

Rachel smiled sleepily and said, 'I know it's rather beastly of me but I think I'll go to bed too. And since Helen mentioned it, I'm beginning to feel positively knackered.'

"What? It's early yet, only ten forty-five. How about the three of us have a nightcap?' Sofia asked.

'No, thank you Sofia, I really do think I'll call it a night,' Rachel said, sleepily.

Sofia nodded. 'You are right. I think we could all do with a good night's rest. It's been a long day. I'll just inform Henry and the others that we girls are turning in.'

'Well, goodnight then,' Rachel said as she left the room.

Chapter Nineteen

A t about midnight, Jeremy burst into the room and switched on the light. 'Rachel, wake up! The most awful thing has happened. Rachel, do wake up.'

Rachel sat up in bed, rubbing sleep from her eyes. 'What is it Jeremy? What time is it? And what happened to your dinner jacket?' She asked, noticing his wet, mud splattered clothes.

'Evelyn's dead.'

'What, how?'

'Her car went off the cliff.'

'Oh, dear God!'

'About an hour ago, Constable Goole was bicycling his way upto Falcon's Crest to begin his night duty here, when he saw a car go off the road and over the cliff. He immediately cycled over here and telephoned the police station and the Inspector about the accident he had witnessed. And Sofia had just informed us that Evelyn had taken the Judge's car about ten minutes prior to that and we put two and two together.'

'Then, there's a chance that Evelyn may still be alive,' Rachel said, hoping beyond hope that was the case.

'Afraid not. Antonio, Timothy and I trekked down the cliff and found the car had smashed into a rock below. The car was well and truly mangled. We managed to reach it and found her jammed between the front seat and the steering wheel. We tried but we couldn't extricate her. I checked but there was no pulse and there was a huge gash in her chest where the steering wheel entered her ribcage. She was in a pool of blood. The police are getting metal cutters and I suppose they ought to have her out soon.'

'Ugh, looks like she died on impact. God, this is awful Jeremy, but you had better get out of your clothes, looks like a lot of the blood got on to you.'

'Yes, that must've happened when Antonio and I tried to pull her out.'

'How is he coping?'

'He's devastated. They all are. Timothy and the Judge are downstairs too. We just got back and Sofia has just given them some brandy. I ran up to tell you and ask if you could take a set of my clean clothes down to them, while I change. I think my clothes ought to fit Antonio. Timothy can probably borrow something from John, if mine don't fit.'

'Of course, Jeremy. I'll do it right away. That's the least I can do,' Rachel said as she got out of bed to do the needful.

She padded down in her robe and slippers with a change for the boys. They were all in the library.

Sofia was weeping, 'It's all, my fault. I should have never allowed her to drive back.'

Helen was trying to comfort her, 'Sofia, it's not your fault. Evelyn was so sure about driving back on her own.'

The Judge spoke up in anger, 'This stretch of road is awfully dangerous, especially in the rain and cars have gone over the edge before. There were two accidents just last year. I wrote to the authorities to do something about it but as usual, nothing was done. The administration of this country has well and truly gone to the dogs!'

Sofia was inconsolable. 'See? Everyone knows that road is dangerous. I should have never let her drive back."

Henry Cavendish put his arm around her, 'Darling, please don't blame yourself. Accidents can happen anytime, to anyone.'

Timothy was silent and Antonio sat next to him with his head in his hands.

Rachel quietly went up to them and handed them the folded clothes and told them to change in the washroom down the hall, next to the guest room. As they thanked her and got up to go, John hobbled through the door, using his sticks. 'What's all the commotion about? What's happened?'

II

The next morning, Jeremy received a telephone call from London. It was Duke Wellington.

'Good morning, guv'nor.'

'Good morning, Duke. Did you manage to locate Samuel Reid?'

'Aye, I did.'

'What did he have to say?'

'Nowt, I know of, guv'nor. Chap at the pub told me he'd gone off to Scotland. Had a great big windfall, some time ago and packed his bags and left.'

'Oh! I see. Any idea, where in Scotland?'

'Aye, guv'nor, he left this forwarding address for his pension checks to be sent out. That's why I thought I'd have a word with you. The chap said he's gone back home to his fishing folks in Aberdeen. I found out where it is, and if you want I can take a train upto Edinburgh and then hop on to a train from there to Aberdeen.'

'Why, that's very good thinking, Duke. We'll make a detective out of you, yet. What do you think of an all expenses paid trip to Aberdeen and back?'

'Aye, guv'nor, I'd love to travel and see a bit o' the world. I can get a chum of mine, to drive the taxi for a bit till I get back.'

'Then it's settled. I'll wire a friend of mine at Scotland Yard - a lady, called Marge Harding, and ask her to organise some funds for you on my behalf. Go to Scotland Yard tomorrow at four in the afternoon and ask for her.

And another thing, Duke, we'll double your reward if you can get back with the information within a week from tomorrow.'

Duke whistled and said, "For forty quid! I'd go to hell and back for that kind of brass, guv'nor."

As Jeremy ended his telephone call with Duke, Sofia's maid, Marie informed him that Sofia would like to see him in Captain John Griffin's room, right away.

III

The door to John's room was ajar. Jeremy found John and Sofia deep in conversation as he entered.

'You wanted to see me?' He asked.

Sofia looked up and said, 'Yes, oh, it's just awful but you have to help John.'

'Help John with what?' Jeremy asked with a puzzled expression.

'Detective, my box containing the veronal sachets, is gone!'

'Gone?'

'Gone, disappeared, as in, vanished!'

'When did this happen?'

'I really couldn't say. After all the drinks last night, I didn't take any. I just went to bed and was off to sleep as soon as my head hit the pillow. I only got up hearing all your voices in the middle of the night. When I came back from the library, I couldn't get back to sleep, so I thought I'd take some and I looked about for it but it was gone!'

'When was the last time you took it?'

'Well, I took some the night before last at the hospital.'

'Are you sure you brought it with you from the hospital?'

'Yes. I remember asking Helen to put it on my bedside table, when she was arranging my things.'

'So it could have disappeared any time yesterday, after you settled in.'

'I suppose so.'

'Who else visited you in your room yesterday?'

'Let me think... just you, Sofia, Helen and Rachel and one of the maids must have been in because my bed was turned down when I came back to sleep.'

'Could anyone have come in during the party?'

'Possibly. The door wasn't locked and I was cooped up on the settee in Sofia's sitting room for the better part of the evening.'

'Hmm, so what you're saying is that just about anyone present at the party could have nipped in and taken the box, through the course of the evening.'

'The washroom is right next door, so I suppose most people came by at one time or another to use it, through the evening.'

'Who else knew that you were prescribed Veronal?'

'I suppose everybody who visited me at the hospital knew.'

'So that pretty much includes everybody at the party last night.'

'Yes.'

'Any guesses on who would have taken it?'

'Absolutely none, Detective,' John concluded, shaking his head.

'I think we'd better inform the police about it,' Jeremy said.

Sofia asked, 'Really, Jeremy, do you think that's absolutely necessary? It could turn up or someone may have borrowed some.'

'You could be right, Sofia, although I have my doubts. Surely, if someone wanted to borrow it, they would've asked John first. I suggest we wait and ask everyone, if they know anything about it. But if no one does, we had better inform the police. Administered wrongly, Veronal can be extremely dangerous.'

Chapter Twenty

By four in the afternoon, Doctor Meadows had finished performing the autopsy and the results of the blood and chemical analysis had come in, from his assistant at the laboratory. He was a worried man.

Twenty minutes later, he was at the police station facing Inspector Thomas. He put his autopsy report on his desk and said, 'This was no ordinary accident, Inspector.'

'What?'

'The accident was caused owing to the fact that the victim went off to sleep behind the wheel, Inspector. If she hadn't crashed the car, she would have anyway died in her sleep, upon reaching home. There was enough Veronal in her system to drown an elephant. I think, it is safe to say that Evelyn Belloni's death can be classified under murder in the first degree.'

'Bloody hell!

'My sentiments exactly.'

'But wait a minute. How on earth would anyone in that house, get their hands on Veronal? We removed all potentially poisonous substances from Ravenrock after Edith and Adelaide Wilson's deaths. And Veronal is a prescription drug.'

'Yes, it is. But you are targeting the wrong household. Evelyn Belloni was in all likelihood, poisoned at Falcon's Crest. And you don't have to look far to find Veronal there, Inspector. I only just prescribed it for Captain John Griffin, myself. They shifted him to Falcon's Crest from the hospital, yesterday.'

'That's very interesting but why was he moved to Falcon's Crest?'

'Apparently the Judge's household is in a bit of a disarray, after Edith Wilson died and the Cavendishes offered to take care of the convalescent.'

'Right! I'll be off to question him. In fact, I'm going to question the lot of them.'

'I thought you already did after Edith Wilson and Adelaide's deaths.'

'That was then, now things seem to be a lot clearer. And this time the chap has gone too far and got caught in a web of his own making!'

'So you know who's behind all these deaths?' The doctor asked with a touch of incredulity.

'I wouldn't underestimate police intelligence, if I were you, doctor. We've been doing our bit quietly and on a hunch I got in touch with Inspector Parker and he has friends in the war office. I've just got a wire from him that says that they never had a Mike Murray on active service or on any of their desertion lists. So, if you ask me, Captain John Griffin's tale about knowing him as a deserter from his army days, is just plain old bunkum. In fact, we're about to get the Captain's war records and everything including any file photographs they've got on Captain John Griffin. For all we know, the chap's an imposter.'

'Well, I'll be dashed!'

'Now, if you'll excuse me doctor, I have a murderer to catch.'

II

Inspector Thomas was greeted at the door by Henry Cavendish's valet – Raleigh, who had returned the day before with his master's luggage from London.

'Good evening, Sir.'

'Good evening. Could you please inform Mr. Cavendish that I'd like a word with him, in private.'

'Yes, Sir. The family is taking tea in the sitting room. If you would care to wait in the library I will inform Mr. Cavendish.'

Five minutes later, Henry Cavendish walked into the library. He was casually dressed in a grey trousers and a white shirt.

'Hello, Inspector. Is there any further news about the accident last night?'

'I'm here about that, Mr. Cavendish. I'd like to interview all the members of your household, over the next few days and Captain John Griffin, in particular.'

'Interview us? Regarding the accident, you mean? Surely, you don't suspect any foul play? It was unfortunate, no doubt, but accidents do happen.'

'Not like this one. The autopsy report gives a different story altogether, Mr. Cavendish.'

'Good Lord! You don't say! Did someone run her off the road?'

'Not quite, Sir. The doctor believes she was administered a large amount of Veronal, possibly by someone in this house and the accident was a result of the drug taking its full effect.'

'My God! And John just informed us that his Veronal went missing yesterday.'

'That seems rather convenient. Exactly when did he make this claim?'

'It is all very distressing and confusing, Inspector. I'll just fetch Detective Richards. I daresay, he'll be able to give you a coherent report of what has been going on.'

'Right, and if you could also let the others know that I'd like a word with them.'

'Yes. I will inform everyone. But who on earth would want to kill Evelyn!'

III

Jeremy walked into the library shortly and greeted the Inspector.

'I hear that Evelyn was given Veronal.'

'That's right but what's all this I hear, about the Captain claiming his Veronal went missing yesterday?'

Jeremy updated him on the events of the morning.

The inspector told Jeremy that he had been in touch with Inspector Parker and that Parker had used his contacts in the war office and found out that Mike Murray had never been in the army and their suspicions that Captain John Griffin could be an imposter. He also mentioned that they are expecting complete details on Captain John Griffin's war records, as soon as possible.

'When will Inspector Parker be able to get us the details?'

'By tomorrow, hopefully. He's taking the first train out from London and ought to be back by tomorrow afternoon. Also, based on the tip from your wife, we got in touch with a Mrs. Ansell in Kent to give us any information she has about The Three Oaks Orphanage, where we believe Lucy Jones' children were sent after the trial.'

'Any luck?'

'Oh, yes. Mrs. Ansell informed us over the telephone that the orphanage closed down long before she got married and moved to the village in question but her mother-in-law remembers that while most of the younger children from the orphanage were sent to foster homes and put up for adoption, two of the boys remained at the vicarage with Vicar Griffin – and while she can't remember the younger one's name, upon prodding, she said it may have been something like Michael but she couldn't be sure. However, here's the interesting part - she remembers the older one clearly because he had a peculiar name and it stuck in her mind. She said the boy's name was Dusty Jones.'

'And you think Dusty Jones is ...'

'None other than Captain John Griffin.'

II

Raleigh held the door open as John hobbled into the library with the aid of his crutches. John was looking pale.

'What is it, Inspector?' John asked.

'Do take a seat, Captain. This may take a while, there are certain questions we need to ask you.'

'Right. As you might have heard, I've been very worried ever since my Veronal disappeared and now Mr. Cavendish tells me it was used to kill Evelyn.'

'That is correct. However, the questions I need to ask you are of a different nature and I'll get right down to it, if you are comfortable.'

'I'm comfortable enough,' John said, as he shifted uncomfortably in his seat.

'To begin with Captain, what is your real name?'

'What an odd question – it is John Griffin, of course! But you already know that.'

'Yes. Let me be more specific. Is that the name you were born with?'

'No. I was orphaned early in life and later adopted by Vicar Griffin, who very kindly gave me a home and education, along with his name. But what has that got to do with whatever's been going on here?'

'We believe, this case hinges upon the identity of two boys who were orphaned due to circumstances which involved Judge Wilson. We believe that Mike Murray was one of them and that you happen to be the other one and that your real name is Dusty Jones,' the inspector said, getting down to brass tacks.

'I see,' John said simply.

'Is it true?'

'Well, yes and no.'

'Care to enlighten us?'

'Yes, my name was Darrel Jones. 'Dusty' was a name given to me by other boys at the orphanage, Mike Murray being one of them.'

'And why did you not tell us this before?'

'I didn't think it mattered. And as far as my name goes, you never asked me,' John replied simply.

The inspector was taken aback with the honestly of his response. 'Right. Who was Mike Murray and this time we want the truth. Was he your brother?'

'No, he was not my brother. He was one of the boys from the orphanage and as I told you before, he also was a deserter from the army, from one of my platoons.'

'That's funny because the war office tells us that no one by that name was ever in the army.'

'Then the war office is wrong. He was Lance Corporal Michael Murray Reid and he served in my platoon.'

'We'll see.'

Jeremy spoke at this point, 'Do you know why he came to these parts or what he was doing here?'

'I haven't a clue, Detective. I was just as surprised to see him here, as anyone else.'

The inspector asked, 'One last question – was Judge Wilson aware of your former identity as Darrell Jones?'

'What do you think, Inspector? Since you seem to know all about it?' John asked with a touch of smugness.

Inspector Thomas flared. 'I'll tell you what we think, Mr. Dusty Jones. We think that you entered the Judge's home under false pretences and then went on a killing spree to avenge what you thought was injustice meted out to your family twenty years ago. And that you also killed your brother because you feared that he would reveal your real identity to the Judge and his family.'

'And I suppose I staged the accident that damn near killed me, as well. Why don't you arrest me then? Is it possibly, because you have no basis for your wild accusations, or could it be that you have no proof whatsoever, Inspector?'

'Oh, we'll get proof alright and when we do, I will make sure that you hang for your crimes.'

'I look forward to it. Would that be all for now?'

'Yes, for now. But make no mistake, *I will be back,*' The Inspector said, with menace in his voice as he stalked out of the room.

Henry Cavendish followed the Inspector out of the library.

Jeremy and John looked at each other and Jeremy couldn't help the smile that came to his face.

Jeremy spoke. 'That wasn't a very wise thing to do – getting the Inspector's back up like that. He'll be gunning for you now.'

'He was gunning for me anyhow, Detective. He practically accused me of being a mass murderer!'

'You have a point there. Do *you* have any idea, as to, who could be behind all these deaths?'

'I haven't the faintest. I wish I knew but I'm just as puzzled as anyone else.'

'Tell me, John, if I'm not mistaken, you also had a younger sibling, namely Robin Jones?'

'Yes. But in all honesty, Robin was adopted by another family soon after the orphanage shut down and I have no idea about Robin's current whereabouts.'

'It must have been awfully hard on you, as a child, to lose your family, so suddenly and tragically.'

'Yes, it was. I never thought I would get over it. But life has a plan for all of us, Detective and God works in mysterious ways.'

'Mysterious as his ways may be, it does seem a tad bit orchestrated that you ended up marrying the Judge's daughter.'

'You are sharp, Detective. You see, when I met Pamela during the war, through a stroke of pure coincidence, or as some would put it - through God's mysterious ways, and came to know that she was Judge Wilson's daughter, I had an idea that I could bring shame and ruin upon his family by simply having an affair and leaving her as an unwed mother.'

Jeremy raised his eyebrow. 'But, you obviously didn't.'

'I simply couldn't. You see, I hadn't factored something into the avenging equation. The fact that I would fall deeply and incomprehensibly in love with her. She was an affectionate, bright, upstanding and fine girl. She reminded me so much of my own mother that I just couldn't bring myself to destroy her, irrespective of how I felt about her father. She had a quality of goodness about her, despite being born to a man like Judge Wilson. If you had ever met her you would understand completely, why I could not bring myself to punish her for the sins of her father.'

'And yet, you chose to stay in her father's house – the very man who had destroyed your family. Why is that?'

'Strangely enough, I don't know if you will believe me, but my intention was purely to meet the Judge and the rest of Pamela's family, so that I could visit my wife and child's graves, and then leave. Through a strange twist of fate, and Edith Wilson's intervention, before I knew it, Judge Wilson's family became my family. You see, I found myself in a rather unique situation after the war - I had no one else in the world to call my own, and no other place to call home.'

Chapter
Twenty One

Duke Wellington sighed. Upon reaching Aberdeen, after an arduous journey that had taken him nearly twenty four hours and several misdirections by well meaning Scottish folk, he had finally managed to locate a house given on the slip of paper he had been carrying. All it said was 'Taigh Anna, Footdee,' or 'Fittie' as the locals called it, which Duke learned upon his arrival and consequent wanderings. The small fishing village was located close to the mouth of River Dee in the northeast of Scotland. While it was scenic and he had enjoyed wandering up and down the quaint cobbled lanes, picturesque outhouses and meeting friendly locals, he had already visited four homes called 'Taigh Anna'. His hope of finding Samuel Reid was beginning to wane as he found to his utter dismay that there were more houses named 'Taigh Anna' in the vicinity of Fittie, than you could shake a stick at.

Plus nobody really spoke English in a way he could understand. He had managed so far by showing the piece of paper with Samuel Reid's name and address written on it and all he had heard so far was 'Nae', or 'Cha' followed by a shake of the head, which he presumed meant a 'no' in Scottish and Gaelic. As he stood in front of the fifth stone built cottage, the painted blue door was opened by a short, plump old lady with pink cheeks, who smiled brightly at him and said, 'Halò, dè tha thu ag iarraidh?'

Duke touched his hat, broke into a charming toothy smile and said, 'Hello. I'm sorry ma'am, I don't understand. Anyone speak English at home? As in, E-n-g-l-i-s-h?'

'Aha! Cha! Chan eil beurla agam! Feith! Feith!' she told him cheerfully, in what he presumed was Scottish Gaelic.

'Oh, I get it. You're asking me to wait?'

'Jes, feith!' She said, clapping her hands at his linguistic brilliance. She trotted down the stone path and banged on her neighbour's door. As soon as it opened, she told whoever was standing inside a long story gesticulating towards him from time to time. A young woman stepped out and came towards him. Duke noticed she had big eyes, a good figure and long brown hair tied back with a scarf at the nape of her neck.

'Halo, ken I help ye? Ma grandmaw, she dinnae understand English. She says yer lukin fer someone English?' She asked in a sing song voice.

Duke was smitten at first glance, and as was the case with him, when confronted with a good looking woman, he started stammering. 'Well, er, yes, in a manner of s-s-speaking.'

She looked at him puzzled, 'Nae? Ye isnae looking fer one who speaks English?'

Without much ado, he thrust the piece of paper at her and said, 'I, er, am looking for a bloke, er, I mean, a man, by the name of Samuel Reid', and he thought to himself *...And God have mercy, please let me find him here because I am really, really hungry, half dead and tired of walking about all over this fishing village.*

'Aye, you've come lookin' fer ma grandmaw's brother! But he dun gun out with de fishing boats and ah dinnieken when he'll be back. Mebbe in te evenin.'

'God bless you, lass. I'll come back in the evening, then,' he said, feeling slightly better.

The old lady broke out into a flurry of speech and gesticulated towards him.

'Ma grandmaw wants tae ken whaur ye ar fae.'

'Tell her, I'm f-f-from the grand old city of London and I've come all the way, just to meet her brother. And my name is Duke Wellington.'

The young woman translated and then after hearing what the old lady had to say, she spoke. 'My grandmaw says, ye have travelled a lawng way and ye must be hungry. Would ye like tae rest a wee bit and get summat to eat and drink?'

Duke said, 'Oh, Jes, jes! Tell your grandmamma that s-s-she is an angel from heaven and that I love her dearly.' His feet were aching. A rest and some refreshment was just what he needed.

The young woman giggled and translated.

The old woman put her head back and laughed and then took his face in her hands and gave him resounding kisses on both his cheeks.

She turned around and trotted back up the path and beckoned him into the house.

Duke and the young lady followed with a smile.

'Might I ask, what your beautiful grandma's name is?'

'Aye. Her name is Anna. And see here,' she said pointing to the piece of paper, 'Taigh Anna means Anna's house.'

'Ah, well God bless Anna and Taigh Anna! And what is your name?'

'I am also Anna, named after ma grandmaw.'

'What a grand name! I can see why people around these parts, like it so much. If I ever have a daughter, I'll be sure to call her Anna,' Duke said without stammering. He was beginning to feel more at ease now.

By evening, Duke had been properly pampered by Scottish hospitality to such an extent that he hoped Samuel Reid would take his own sweet time to return home. He had found out that Reid had returned to Scotland after having spent thirty years in England. Young Anna told him that after his adopted son - Mike died, he had no family left in England and wanted to come back home and spend his old age with his sister, the older Anna, her grandmother. He and young Anna's father had gone fishing up River Dee, in her father's boat and sometimes they could take upto two days, if not more to return when the weather was good. Their family supplied fish to the local market. She proudly informed him that apart from trout, conger eels and mackerel, their River Dee's spring salmon was in such great demand that it was sent directly by rail to Billingsgate fish market in London.

Duke tried to ask Anna about Mike but she said she had only met him once, when she had travelled to London with her father, as a child. She told him that all she knew about Mike, was what she had heard from her great uncle, and he had told them that Mike had fought in the war and though he survived the war, he had died recently in England.

As the evening wore on, Samuel Reid had not returned, Duke offered to take them both out for a meal and they walked to a quaint seaside restaurant, close by, where they were plied with huge quantities of the fresh catch of the day. The restaurant had five tables of which two were occupied by local fishing folk and Anna informed him that the third table on the far right was occupied by a trio of American marine biologists who had come all the way to study the salmon in River Dee.

Despite the language barrier, he was enjoying the company of both the Annas immensely. They communicated with expressions and gestures as much as they did with their voices. Duke entertained both the Annas by enacting some lively anecdotes about his life in London as a taxi cab driver through the course of the meal.

They ate well, and laughed heartily as a strain of melody coloured the backdrop of their conversation, and music wafted up from the battered old gramophone that sat in one corner of the restaurant. By the time they were through and Duke had paid the bill, Grandma Anna offered to put him up for the night and Duke accepted her hospitality gratefully.

Strangely, in this lonely, windswept corner of the world, in a land where he barely understood the local dialect, he felt more at home than he had ever felt, in any other place on God's green earth.

II

Samuel Reid finally arrived the day after. As his fishing boat docked to the sound of a hundred seagulls flapping around and squawking for their share of haul, he stepped onto the quay and got word from another fisherman that a man from London was awaiting him at his house. News travels fast in small towns and even faster in a village the size of Fittie. As he walked back home, a thousand thoughts ran through his mind. He wondered what this Englishman had come, all the way, for. And he wondered if it had anything to do with Mike's death. He remembered the last time someone had wanted to know about his boy. He wished that he had never spoken to the lady who rang him from Dartmouth and asked all those questions about his adopted son. She had offered both Samuel and Mike a great deal of money to visit her at Dartmouth. Despite Samuel's warnings, Mike had gone for the money. Something had told him then that it would bring bad luck and it did. A week later his boy was found dead. Now, he would just have to wait and see what tidings this stranger had brought him.

Chapter Twenty Two

Jeremy popped his head into their room and found Rachel seated at the window, staring out at the path on the cliffs with a book lying open on her lap. She seemed lost in thought.

'I thought I'd find you here... a penny for your thoughts,' he said.

She turned her head and smiled at him. 'I'd prefer a pound. I'm thinking deep thoughts.'

'My kingdom at your feet, m'lady,' he said, with a wave of his arm.

She put the book away as he pulled up a chair and sat facing her.

Rachel smiled. 'Oh, they aren't *that* valuable. So what did the inspector have to say?'

'I'll tell you everything but first let's go for a walk. Some fresh air might do us both some good.'

Ten minutes later, Jeremy and Rachel found themselves walking along the cliff road. As they walked, Jeremy brought her up to date on the Inspector's findings and the subsequent grilling that John had undergone, in the library.

Rachel was taken aback. 'So, John is Lucy Jones' son. That is a surprise. And obviously the Judge hasn't guessed, or has he?'

'I have a feeling that John had a premonition - that his secret would come out during the course of this investigation. To my mind, that's probably one of the main reasons why he wasn't too keen on going back to Ravenrock.'

'I don't blame him. But something else is bothering me. I had assumed that it was one of the Jones children who were behind these murders. This kind of throws my theory into the water because I don't think John is the killer anymore than you do.'

'But let's not forget that he did have access to the veronal and motive to boot. And he could have easily committed all the murders barring Adelaide's. He is the most likely suspect, in the eyes of the law but, somehow, I too get a strange feeling that he is not our murderer.'

'No.' Rachel said, 'Let's look at it from a different point of view. All along, we've been going with the theory that the motive behind these murders is vengeance. What if it's not? What if it is, in fact something silly like money or property? Aside from John, why don't we check on who stands to gain if all or most of the stake holders to the Judge's will are eliminated one by one?'

'Hmm, very interesting. That would bring Timothy and Antonio on top of our suspect's list. I think I'll request the Inspector to run a background check on the contents of the Judge's will and Timothy and Antonio's individual financial standing. If both or either is in debt, it will be useful to know.'

Rachel said, 'And between you and me, I know for a fact that Antonio has a roving eye. He may even have a mistress or two tucked away somewhere.'

Jeremy raised an eyebrow and Rachel hastened to explain. 'I know this for a fact because the night you were away at London, he tried his very best to charm the socks off me but don't worry - just like Marge Harding, I told him very sternly to change his 'rakish ways'! Of course, it could just be a side effect of being Italian and a race car driver on top of that, but I'm not so sure.'

'Interesting. And I agree, it may be worth our while to delve a little deeper into Antonio's personal life to see if he had any additional motive to get rid of his wife. With so many murders taking place, it would be the easiest thing for any opportunist to get rid of his spouse, without drawing direct attention to oneself as a prime suspect. Knowing full well that most people, the police included, would be busy looking in the other direction, trying to solve the spate of murders, as we have been.'

They walked for a while in silence lost in their own thoughts till they reached a point where the high grass on the side of the road was flattened down. Jeremy stopped to point out the place where Evelyn's car had gone off the road. Rachel stepped forward towards the edge and peered down. Despite the steep incline, she could see the remains of the Judge's car. She shuddered.

'How on earth did you boys manage to get to it, without breaking your necks?'

'It was raining that night. All we could see were the car's headlights shining through the rain, in the distance. Luckily, we had flashlights to find our way in the dark. And we could only see three feet beyond, at a time. Plus, the knowledge that Evelyn may still have been alive and badly hurt, spurred us on. Had it been daylight, I doubt if any of us would have had the courage to make it all the way down there, without safety ropes.'

Rachel was pensive. 'What an awful way to die. I don't care if the doctor claims she was asleep at the wheel when it happened. No matter how drugged she may have been, there must have been a moment of wide eyed terror as she plummeted down to her death.'

'Quite possibly.'

'I just wish we could just stop these terrible things from happening,' Rachel said looking out over the horizon as River Dart twinkled below.

Jeremy spoke, 'You've been awfully quiet the past couple of days. Is there something else on your mind, darling?'

'You mean, aside from watching helplessly while people around us get murdered?'

'Yes, I'm beginning to think that there's something bothering you deeply and yet it's not like you to keep anything from me. You do know, that I'll try and be as understanding as possible and anything you tell me, will stay between us unless you want it otherwise.'

'Of course, Jeremy.'

'So, what is it then?'

'It's just something that crossed my mind the other day. It's nothing, really. And now that John has admitted to being Lucy Jones' son, the theory I've been mulling over the past few days, no longer holds water because it simply cannot be. But I must admit, it is a load off my mind, for whatever his confession is worth. I think all this detecting business is getting on my nerves and making me delusional.'

'Darling, it is hard, I know, especially since this case involves old friends and people you've come to like.'

'I certainly don't like the Judge. I think he's a pompous old stuffed shirt without a conscience and I can just see him going about murdering anyone who comes in his way. He's done it before, Jeremy, and if I've learnt anything about human nature, it is the fact that *people don't change.* Oh, they may talk differently, dress differently and behave differently over time but intrinsically, people don't change.'

'You can't be serious.'

'It's true. Think about it. Good people remain good no matter what life throws at them. For example, John could have easily ruined Pamela's life when he had the chance but he just couldn't because there is a certain goodness about him. He was born with it. No matter how bitter, how hurt or how strong his reasons were he could not carry out his vengeance. Whereas, the Judge , on the other hand...'

'Yes, I do get what you're trying to say, and it's interesting, but people do change, darling. I have seen people change. I've changed. Circumstances can change people.'

'No, Jeremy. Only superficial qualities change. I strongly believe that the essence that you are, never changes. Circumstances can only magnify or diminish your essence but it will remain the same throughout one's life. For example, if there is evil or cruelty in one's essence, it will come through, at the slightest provocation and if there is good, it will shine through, irrespective of the provocation.'

'You sound just like my Sunday school teacher, darling.'

'Oh God, I hope not! I'm not trying to be the least bit moralistic, or judgemental for that matter, darling – I am just trying to explain my philosophy to you. And in my own harebrained way, what I am trying to say, is that there is a basis to my instinct that John is not the killer. I suppose it is based entirely on my theory that people don't change, but there it is.'

'I know one thing that's never going to change – the way you continue to surprise me, every step of the way. Now here's a thought for you – for the better part of my adult years, I never thought I'd marry or even enjoy being married and now I can't imagine living my life without you or your charming, harebrained ideas. Now if that isn't change, I don't know what is!'

Chapter
Twenty Three

Inspector Parker had returned from London. He met up with Jeremy and Rachel at the cafe. He had done his due diligence and found out a great deal about the Judge and John Griffin.

'As it turns out, inside information tells us that Judge Wilson had an impeccable scandal free record up until the case with Jones. He was reputed to be a clean professional with family values. Not a closet 'ladies' man', as we first suspected, so this was definitely an aberration in his behaviour. Now, don't get me wrong, I'm not campaigning for his character but something tells me that there's more to the Jones' case than meets the eye. It's a very remote possibility but insider sources tell me that the general impression, at the time was that he could have been framed. Although he may have got off Scott-free in legal terms, it did do his reputation a great deal of harm and negatively impacted the remainder of his career.'

Rachel exclaimed, 'I'm glad! There is justice in the world after all!'

Jeremy said, 'Aren't you being a tad bit harsh on the man, dear? Granted, that he may have behaved irresponsibly with Lucy Jones and her children but, to have your entire reputation and the remainder of your career destroyed, and then your family murdered, for one aberration, seems a rather harsh form of medieval justice.

Inspector Parker spoke, 'I couldn't agree more. Fact is, that Bedlow conveniently left out an important titbit, in his narration to you that both the Judge and the ex-footman were grilled intensively by officers at the time, until they found out conclusively that Judge Wilson had nothing to do with Lucy Jones' unfortunate railway accident. As it turns out, it seems to have been one of those bizarre coincidences that one of the eye witnesses had previously been in the Judge's employ.'

Rachel said, 'That may be so but it does not make the Judge any less guilty, in my eyes. And Jeremy, you of all people, ought to know that if we all held the belief that one aberration didn't count, the law of our land wouldn't send people who commit single murders to the gallows!'

Jeremy replied, 'Yes, dear, but one must keep in mind that he did not commit murder – single or otherwise, and now it does seem as though we may have read too much into Bedlow's narration. I reckon, there is no point in getting emotional about it, we need to be cool and practical to get to the bottom of this.' Turning to Inspector Parker he then asked, 'What about John Griffin? You did say you delved into his army records?'

'Yes, as a matter of fact, John Griffin's war records checked out just fine. I double checked against the photographs on file. He is, who he says he is. The war office also has it on record that he is the son of one Vicar William Griffin of Kent.'

'Adopted son. John confessed yesterday to Inspector Thomas that he is Lucy Jones' son, and that he was later adopted by Vicar Griffin.'

'Oh! I see. That is interesting,' said inspector Parker.

'Yes, but I still can't see him as our murderer. He would have had to be a Houdini; to be in two places at once, if he committed Adelaide's murder. Everything tells me that we are close, very close, and that perpetrator is someone we know well, but I still haven't a clue as to who our mysterious killer is.

II

The inquest was held on Friday. Dr. Meadows gave his statement followed by P.C. Goole and Inspector Thomas. Jeremy, Antonio and Timothy also gave statements as to what condition they had found the body of the deceased in. The verdict returned was, 'Death by murder by person or persons unknown. The media had gone into a frenzy as reporters and editors across the land began to connect the dots. One of the tabloids had gone as far as to uncover the Judge's old case. The Sunday paper's headline screamed, 'Sordid past comes back to haunt Hon'ble Judge Wilson.'

The tabloid gave a colourful account of the Jones case, the consequent sentencing for attempted murder and followed by Lucy Jones' mysterious suicide and the tragic consequences upon their children. Jeremy was surprised to see a detailed account of Tom Bedlow's statement in the same tabloid that went on to describe how sorry he had felt for the children, at the time. Jeremy realised that Bedlow was gunning for the Judge and doing his best to get long overdue justice for Lucy Jones' known surviving child – John Griffin. While there was tremendous sympathy for John Griffin, it was equally evident that the public had already pinned the Dartmouth murders on him.

A day later, under immense pressure from the media and authorities, Inspector Thomas had no other recourse but to arrest John Griffin on murder charges.

Most of the tabloids carried a file picture of Captain John Griffin in uniform and also questioned why his father, Cyril Jones had been sentenced and sent to Dartmoor on a relatively lesser charge of attempted murder. The article went on to describe the conditions of Dartmoor Prison in the early 1920s and that it had contained some of the most serious offenders of that time. One of the most prominent papers even went on to ask the question in its headlines – 'Like father, like son?' and another headline read, 'Avenging Fury, Son-in-law Arrested.'

Tabloids carried photographs of the Judge's entire family that it sourced from different places. Adelaide's school picture taken a year ago, Edith's photo from the local horticultural society magazine, a file picture of Antonio and Evelyn at a racing event, Timothy's picture from the Dartmouth Royal Regatta held the year before. And finally a grainy photo of Judge Wilson leaving the inquest holding his hand up at the camera, as if trying to shoo the cameraman away. The caption under it read, *'Reclusive Judge Wilson, shies away from Judgement Day.'*

With all the press and publicity involved, Jeremy had a notion that the old case would definitely be re-looked at, if not officially re-opened. Either way, he was certain about one thing – both John Griffin and the Hon'ble Judge Wilson were in for a rough time and that whatever the outcome, their lives would never be the same again.

III

The team from Scotland Yard had arrived in Dartmouth. Jeremy was requested to be present at the police station.

Chief Inspector Harrow addressed him. 'I should have known, you and Bedlow were onto something when you came sniffing around. Why didn't you tell me it was related to the Dartmouth murders?'

'Back then, I wasn't so sure about it myself, Chief Inspector. As you put it, quite correctly, at that point in time, that's all I was doing, sniffing around.'

'Anyhow, I'm glad you haven't been singing about it to the press, the way Bedlow has.'

'I wasn't aware Bedlow was singing,' Jeremy said, with a herculean effort to maintain a straight face, unable to picture Bedlow with any singing talent whatsoever.

'Like a canary in a coal mine, Detective. Don't tell me you haven't been reading the papers. Remind me to have a word with him about it.'

'Right, Chief Inspector,' Jeremy said out loud... *And that'll be the end of his musical career,* he thought to himself, smiling inwardly.

'So, what do you think? It seems to be a pretty straight forward case.'

'I wish I could share your optimism, Chief Inspector, however, I have my reservations about John Griffin being the murderer.'

'Why am I not surprised?' Inspector Harrow said wearily.

'According to the facts of the case, he has the perfect alibi for one of the murders. He could not have possibly killed the child, Adelaide.'

'And there is no possibility that the child drowned by accident? The medical report does say that she had water in the lungs.'

Jeremy knew that in the short time that Chief inspector Harrow had taken over the case, he had already done his homework thoroughly and gone into every detail of the case files. On this particular point, he had to agree. 'There is that remote possibility but owing to the fact that she was also drugged, I wouldn't read too much into the fact that she had water in the lungs. I definitely believe she was murdered, Chief.'

'There seems to be a pattern here. It looks as though our murderer's objective was to make all the deaths look like accidents. First an accidental overdose of sleeping powders, followed by two accidental drowning cases - that of the girl and that man, Mike Murray and then a car accident.'

'Yes but let's not forget that John Griffin himself was a victim of a car accident and was nearly killed.'

'Or should we say, conveniently survived?'

'You think, that accident was staged to pull the wool over our eyes?'

'Well, it doesn't take a genius to crash a car into a tree and cut the brakes afterwards.'

'Wouldn't the genius also make sure that he got off without broken bones?'

'Not necessarily, broken bones give him some added credibility, I grant you that but we are not dealing with a sane person here. Irrefutable fact being that he was the only one who survived an alleged murder attempt and that makes me suspicious.'

'And his alibi for Adelaide's death?

'It may be that he is working in tandem with someone else. And we just need to find out who it is.'

At that moment, Inspector Thomas walked in to his room waving a piece of paper and said, 'That may not be necessary, gentlemen. What I have here, is a bonafide signed confession from the suspect, confessing to all the murders. Open and shut case, I'd say.'

'Congratulations, Inspector Thomas, you seem to have done it.' The Chief Inspector got up with a new found respect in his eyes and held his hand out to Thomas.

As the men shook hands, Jeremy was bewildered but managed to say, 'Yes, that's quite a coup! You would have had a hell of a time proving he was the murderer based only on circumstantial evidence. This changes everything.'

'I told you I'll make sure he hangs. Once I knew, he was the Jones boy, it was just a matter of time before I got the bugger.'

Jeremy asked, 'May I read the confession?'

'Certainly, I'll have a copy sent over to Falcon's Crest. Meanwhile, the Chief Inspector and I need to address certain members of the press who are eagerly awaiting news on the case. If you'll excuse us, we'll get right to it.'

'By all means,' Jeremy said, as he made way for them.

Chapter
Twenty Four

'No! I don't believe it! I can't and I won't. Henry, please get him a good lawyer. I bet they've beaten the confession out of him.' Sofia was distraught.

Henry tried to calm her down, 'Darling, please. We are in England, not in the Wild West! And this is not a Hollywood motion picture. The police simply don't beat people into making confessions here.'

Jeremy spoke up, 'I have to agree with Henry on this, Sofia. It seems he has confessed of his own free will without any form of coercion on anybody's part. It's almost as if he has a death wish.'

'Why do you say that?' Henry Cavendish asked.

'Because he had a very real chance of being acquitted. The case against him is based entirely on a house of circumstantial cards, and the prosecution would have had to work really hard to prove he committed the murders. His confession however, changes everything.'

'Then you also don't believe that he committed the murders?'Sofia asked.

'No,' Jeremy said simply.

Henry Cavendish paled. 'Do you think he's trying to shield the real murderer?'

'It would seem so.'

'But why on earth would he do that?' Sofia asked baffled.

'I don't know, but I'm going to do my best to find out before it's too late.'

II

Rachel was at Ravenrock. She had felt compelled to speak to Timothy. The Judge had gone into hibernation and was nowhere to be seen. The events of the past few days had hit him hard. Timothy and she sat facing each other, in the Judge's study.

'Timothy, please be careful.'

'Why? You think I'll be the next to go?'

'I hope not but don't you see, you are the only blood relative left. Someone has successfully and mercilessly targeted the rest of your family. '

'What do you expect me to do? Hide in a corner somewhere and hope that the killer doesn't get me?'

'Not quite. Just be alert. Be watchful. And keep this with you at all times,' she said, handing over Sofia's Colt 32 to him.

'You can't be serious. Where did you get this?'

'It's Sofia's. We both thought that under the circumstances, it would be better if you kept it. Look, trust no one. The killer is probably someone you know well and interact with on a regular basis.'

'But haven't you heard? John has confessed to the crimes.'

'What? When?'

'Half an hour ago, apparently. Just before you arrived, we got a call from Inspector Thomas. He called to let father know that John confessed to the murders.'

'I see. Although, I still find it hard to believe that it was John all along.'

'I can't say I blame the poor deranged chap entirely, after learning the misery of a life he's been through. And to think my father was responsible for it.'

'Yes. It is rather sad but that does not excuse the murder of four innocent people,' she said.

'I'm no judge but I wonder why he didn't finish the job properly. I mean, I'm still around. Anyway, it's all over now, so I won't be needing this, after all,' he said, putting the gun back in her hand. 'Besides, John's old service revolver should be around here somewhere,' he said, getting up to open a desk drawer and pulling it out. 'See? I have a gun should I want to use one.'

'Oh, alright. But do keep it next to you,' Rachel said. 'At least until we are absolutely certain that it was him.'

'Thank you Rachel, but it couldn't possibly be anyone else. No one else had any reason to kill my family. I am touched that you and Sofia were so concerned about me.'

Rachel's eyes fell upon a family picture resting on the shelf behind him. 'Who is that girl, in the picture over there?'

Timothy turned around to look at it. 'That's Adelaide. And sitting next to her, is Aunt Edith. This picture was taken at the beginning of summer. We had all gone on a picnic to the Falcon Crest Cove. It was a good day. Idyllic almost. None of us knew then, what the future held for us. We all look so happy and carefree.'

'She looks so different from her picture in the papers. So grown up.'

'Oh, that picture of hers' in the newspapers was an old school photograph, taken a year or so back. This is how she looked before she died. This is how I'll always remember her.'

'And the lady next to her, you said, was Edith.'

'Yes.'

Rachel's mind was in a whirl. Where had she seen those faces before? And since they did not bear a striking resemblance to the grainy images in the newspaper, it could not be there. Then it dawned on her. She got up and with an ashen face, told Timothy, 'Look. I can't explain now but listen carefully, John is not the killer. Keep the gun with you. Stay indoors. No matter who visits, do not let anyone in. I have to go now, there's something I need to do urgently.'

'You can't expect me to sit around and do nothing after a speech like that. For whatever it's worth, I'm coming with you.'

'Alright. Come along then but I have to warn you that you'll be putting yourself in unnecessary danger, if you do.'

'I've lost most of my family to this lunatic. If you think I'm going to sit around and do nothing while you go and confront the killer, you've got another thing coming,' Timothy said, as he followed Rachel out.

III

Jeremy was pacing up and down. He wondered where Rachel had gone. Constable Goole had dropped off the copy of John's confession and he read carefully through it. The confession did not dwell upon how he had managed to kill Adelaide, despite his watertight alibi. He simply said that he had killed her along with the others because it was part of his plan to avenge his parents' deaths. And that he was of sound mind at the time of his confession. It was all too pat. There were too many loose ends and Jeremy disliked loose ends.

Sofia's maid knocked discreetly and entered. 'Sir, there is a telephone call for you from Scotland. Madame has instructed me to ask, if you would care to take it in Mr. Cavendish's sitting room as hers is occupied,' she said.

'Yes! By jove, yes, I would! Thank you Marie,' Jeremy said as he sprinted out the door and up the stairs much to the maid's astonishment. This was just what he needed – the information Duke could give him, straight from the horse's mouth.

'Hello? Duke?'

'Good afternoon, guv'nor.'

'Duke, did you meet Samuel Reid?'

'Did I ever? And do I have news for you. I think you had better sit down, guv'nor. This is going to surprise you.'

'I am sitting down. Duke, don't keep me in suspense. Tell me everything you've learnt from Reid. Time is of the essence.'

Duke did, in detail. Jeremy heard him out in silence. By the end of Duke's narration, they spoke for another minute or so and Jeremy thanked him and hung up. His hands had gone quite cold. He had to find Rachel.

He went straight to Sofia's sitting room and asked her if she had seen Rachel.

Sofia told him that Rachel had come in and asked for Helen, a few minutes ago. 'You'll find her in Helen's studio with Timothy.'

'What's Timothy doing here?'

'I don't know. All I know is that they were headed towards the studio.'

'Right. Where's Henry?'

'In the library. Why?'

'Sofia, get Henry to call the police and come directly to the studio. Bring your gun with you.'

'Oh, but I don't have my gun. Rachel gave it to Timothy.'

'Whatever for? Bloody hell.'

'What's going on? Tell me, Jeremy.'

'There isn't time. I'll explain everything, just call the police and bring Henry and come to the studio. Now!'

'What do I tell the police?'

'To get here as soon as they can. We know who the murderer is and it's not John.'

Jeremy left Sofia gaping as he hurried to the studio. *He thinks its Timothy,* she thought to herself as she went to get her husband.

Chapter Twenty Five

'Why! That's Adelaide! What a beautiful sculpture, Helen,' Timothy said, as Rachel uncovered the sculpture. They had walked in quietly.

Helen whipped around. 'Timothy, Rachel, what are you doing? Both of you, out! Can't you see I'm working?' She had been busy moulding clay into a torso shape.

Rachel said nonchalantly, 'Oh, don't mind us. I just brought Timothy in here, to see your work.'

'I don't want my work seen yet, at least not until it's ready to be exhibited. Now, I love you both but please leave,' Helen said with a touch of irritation.

Before either of them could react, Jeremy opened the door of the sculpting shed and walked in.

Helen spoke. 'Now what? The more the merrier? Why don't I just bring out the wine glasses and we can pretend we're at the exhibit!' She said, rolling her eyes. 'Look, I appreciate that Rachel is proud of my work and wants to show the world but now is not the time,' Helen said.

Jeremy said, 'I'm not here to see your work, Helen. Rachel give me the gun.' He had noticed that Rachel's pocket had a bulge and was relieved that the gun was still with her.

'No, Jeremy. You don't understand,' Rachel pleaded.

'Rachel, give me the gun. *Now.* Thank you,' he said, as Rachel handed the Colt to him. 'And Timothy, if you would care to move towards the table and keep your hands where I can see them.'

'What on earth?' Timothy asked, baffled.

'Just do as you're told and no one will get hurt,' Jeremy said, in a no nonsense voice.

'Can someone please tell me, what the hell is going on?' Helen asked plaintively.

Jeremy's next words were revealing. 'Timothy, the game is over. Do you want to tell them or should I?'

Timothy answered. 'I don't know what you're talking about. Have you gone completely mad?'

At that moment, Sofia and Henry Cavendish walked in and added to the confusion.

Sofia asked, 'What's going on?'

Timothy started shouting. 'I don't know but the detective seems to have gone mad. Henry, help me, He's waving a gun at me!'

'Not until I know what you're doing here, Timothy,' Henry said pointedly.

'His wife tricked me into coming here. She made up some cock and bull story about knowing who the killer was so they could corner me here. For God's sake, get that gun away from him.'

Jeremy said, 'I just got a call from Scotland. Remember Samuel Reid, Timothy?'

'I don't know what the hell you're talking about. I don't know any Samuel Reid.'

'Really, Timothy? Now Samuel had an interesting story to tell us. He told me, that eighteen years ago, Robin Jones, who was seven at the time, was adopted by a well to do Englishman who later moved to Dartmouth. That would make Robin a twenty five year old man by now. It didn't take me long to figure out that it was you he was talking about.'

'Really? So now, at the age of twenty five, I learn from you that I'm adopted? I don't think so.'

Jeremy hissed back, 'I don't think so either. I think you've known all along that you were adopted. No wonder you're the only person who survived. To top it, you're ready to let your brother hang for your dastardly crimes. '

Rachel spoke up at this point. In a quiet understated voice she said, 'Jeremy, please give me the gun. There's no point waving it, at him. You see, you've got it all wrong. It's not Timothy.' She walked up to him and firmly took the gun from him. She continued, 'Robin Jones is and always has been a girl. John had a little sister, rather, has a little sister who he still loves very much. So much so that he's willing to go to the gallows, no questions asked, just to protect her. And Samuel Reid was right. Robin was adopted by a well to do Englishman but it wasn't Judge Wilson. It was Henry Cavendish. Isn't that right, Henry?'

Sofia spoke up, as if coming out of a daze, 'Is it true? Henry, tell me it's not true!'

Henry Cavendish had gone white. But he stayed quiet.

Rachel spoke. 'It's true, Sofia. Why do you think he was so upset when he heard you were going to have a baby? I'll tell you why. Because he and his first wife, Theodora, tried for years and remained barren. They finally adopted a little girl called Robin, whom they renamed Helen. He left you when you told him that you were pregnant and came back to you only after the test results came in, from one of those new fangled fertility clinics in Switzerland. They informed him that he was medically fit and that the problem must have been with his first wife's inability to conceive. Because that's where he spent the better part of two weeks when he told you he was in London. And that's why he couldn't contact you while he was there. The operator would have informed you where the call was coming from. And he didn't want you to know that he was in a clinic in Switzerland. You see, before he had the test results in his hand, he probably entertained the thought that you had been unfaithful and that you were carrying another man's child.'

Sofia spoke slowly, 'My God! I don't believe it but wait a minute, if that's true, Henry would've known all along that Helen could have been Lucy Jones' daughter and she was killing all those people and he never said a word. Why, Henry?'

Henry had silent tears rolling down his face. 'You don't know yet what it's like to love a child with all your heart. I've loved Helen beyond reason. From the day I first set eyes on her. She was so tiny, so scared and lost, I promised myself that I would protect her against anyone and anything. I just couldn't protect her from herself.' Then he turned towards Helen and said, 'Why Helen? How could you? And that too, after I gave you everything any child could want.'

Helen answered, her voice shaking, 'Things! All the things in the world couldn't make up for my mother. Did you think, giving me things would make me forget my mama? Do you have any idea what it's like to be whisked away, taken almost overnight, from a loving home filled with laughter and warmth to a cold orphanage, into a dark and scary, loveless dormitory? Being taunted by other children, every single day, for two long years, that my dead parents – the same parents I loved so much, were murderers and worse. My mother was an angel– the way she would sing to me, tell me bedtime stories and heal every hurt with a kiss. You people probably can't even begin to imagine, what it's like to lose the only person you have ever loved with all your heart. The Judge is only getting what he deserves; he needs to feel the same pain that he put me through. I will not stop until I've killed every single person he loves. Can't you see? That monster has to suffer for all his misdeeds.'

Sofia spoke. 'But, Helen! Adelaide was a motherless child too. How could you kill her so heartlessly?'

'Heartless? Me? When she was stupid enough to go about making announcements to you all that would give our little game away.'

'What little game?' Timothy asked.

'You are not very bright, are you Timothy? How did you think I killed Edith when I never went anywhere near Ravenrock that day? I got that stupid child to do it. Gave her the Veronal and told her it would be such a lark to put the 'laughing powder' into grim Edith's glass. The idiot did it and then got worried the next day because Edith died.'

'So you put her in a bathing suit and drowned her?' Timothy asked, almost shouting.

Helen hissed back. 'You are really very stupid. She was already in a bathing suit modelling for my sculpture. I gave her the same thing mixed with tea in my flask and told her we would need to go down to the cove, so I could do some preliminary sketches to get the windblown hair right. She followed me down like a lamb and as soon as the drug began to work, all I had to do was shove her into the water. Piece of cake!

Jeremy ventured to ask, 'But you couldn't possibly have killed Mike Murray that easily.'

'Mike Murray was a fool, tried to blackmail John. John had told me Mike was coming across on the ferry to collect his money. All I had do to, was lie in wait for him as he got off the ferry and follow him. Then I crept up behind him and hit him with a stout stick. He was drunk anyway and went down like a sack of potatoes. The only difficult part was dragging him to the edge of the path and pushing him off the cliff. He made quite a splash as he hit the water. Luckily no one was about so no one heard anything. Later I put some Italian lire in his holdall, which I had kept aside, and placed it in one of the bushes near the cove. I had hoped the police would find it and suspicion would fall on Antonio and hopefully they would hang him for his murder.'

Rachel said, 'But when the police didn't fall for that ruse, you cut the brakes in his car but that plan backfired as well, didn't it?'

'How was I to know that John would choose that very day to go on a joyride? Anyhow, I've had enough of all this.' Helen suddenly stepped forward and wrenched the gun out of Rachel's unsuspecting hand and pointed it at them. She addressed Henry. 'Daddy, let's go. The rest of you stand back or I'll shoot. I mean it. I've killed before and I have no qualms in killing again. Daddy, come.'

Henry hung his head down, 'It's no good, pudding. I'm afraid, I can't go with you. It's all over.'

'Fine! I hope you all rot in hell. Just don't follow me. I will shoot.'

Rachel appealed to her, 'Helen, it doesn't have to be this way. Give yourself up and we'll get you the best lawyer in the land, I promise.'

Helen hissed back, 'What makes you think, I'm going to trust a rat fink friend like you. You've turned out to be the worst of the lot. You deserve to die more than all the others.'

'No, Helen. Please.' Rachel moved towards her with her arms outstretched and Helen pulled the trigger. The shot rang out as Rachel collapsed in a heap and Helen made a dash for it.

Chapter Twenty Six

Chief Inspector Harrow had accompanied Inspector Thomas and his team to Falcon's Crest. His curiosity was piqued. They had received an almost hysterical telephone call from Henry Cavendish's wife, Sofia, telling them that John was not the killer and that Detective Richards was sure it was Timothy Wilson and that Richards had gone unarmed to confront him, in her step daughter's sculpting shed, in their back garden. He remembered her last words. 'Oh, do come before there's any more bloodshed, Inspector, or this time, it will be on your head.' He had assured her that they would be on their way as soon as possible.

Inspector Thomas had told the Chief Inspector about the call. 'I wouldn't worry too much. It's probably a false alarm.

These actresses can be quite high strung, Chief Inspector, but I suppose I had better look in and see what all the fuss is about.'

'I think I'll tag along, if you don't mind,' had been the Chief Inspector's response. He was just as curious to see what was going on at Falcon's Crest. He had the notion that Detective Richards had not been convinced that John Griffin was the killer. And his past experience with Richards told him that there could be some truth in it. He remembered that, back in the old days, when Richards was part of Scotland Yard, he had been given the nickname 'bull terrier' by his colleagues owing to the fact that he was unstoppable, when he was on the scent of a killer.

They reached Falcon's Crest within fifteen minutes. As soon as they entered the gate, they had heard a gunshot coming somewhere from the back of the house and headed in that direction. They heard the sound of running feet on the gravel path. A terrified young girl had come into view, running with the wind in her hair. As she saw them, she stopped dead in her tracks, raised the gun in her hand and shot at them. All hell broke loose. As they dived to the ground, Inspector Thomas shouted, 'Stop firing. Police!' She took a few more shots at them, as she ran past their prostrated figures and shouted, 'Don't follow me or I'll kill you.' She ran a few yards more till she saw two constables come through the gate, blocking her exit. Inspector Thomas shouted, 'Stop her, Constable! Watch out! She's got a gun!' Cornered and almost out of bullets, she faltered and then froze like a deer caught in headlights. Then as if in slow motion, she turned the gun on herself and fired once, into her right temple. It was the only shot she didn't miss.

II

The press had gone mad. It seemed as though the country's entire fourth estate had descended on to Dartmouth. This case would make history. Chief Inspector Harrow had given a carefully worded press release explaining the circumstances of the Helen Cavendish's, alias Robin Jones' suicide. And that John Griffin was a free man once more. As they let him out of his cell, Constable Goole escorted him out the back door of the police station to avoid the press camped out in front.

John had no idea where he could go from there. It was as if life had played the same old cruel trick on him again. He felt heartsick. To add to his misery, it was raining. As he hobbled out the door with the help of his crutch, Constable Goole pointed to a black car parked discretely on the other side of the lane and told him to get into it as quickly as he could. John was too tired to argue and did as he was told. As he hobbled across and entered the back seat, to his surprise, he found that he shared the seat with Judge Wilson. Timothy was in the driver's seat and Antonio was in the front passenger seat beside him.

No one said anything. As John sat awkwardly and pulled in his crutch to shut the car door, Judge Wilson spoke kindly. 'We thought you could use some help to get back home, son.' He placed his hand on John's hand and patted it. Then in his usual gruff tone, he told Timothy, 'Are you planning to sit here all night, Timothy?'

As Timothy put the car in gear, the two men looked at each other and John said quietly, 'Thank you, Marcus.' John was fighting hard to hold back the tears that threatened to flow.

'It's Dad – as long as you boys are under my roof, you call me Dad,' he said gruffly.

John smiled and said, 'Thanks, Dad.'

III

The next morning, after breakfast, Judge Wilson asked John to come into his study.

As John entered, Judge Wilson motioned him to take a seat opposite him and said, 'The last few weeks have forced me to revisit my past and the consequences my actions have had on you and the lives of many, your sister and my children included. I think I owe you an explanation.'

John nodded. 'And I, you. I'd like to clarify why I had kept the truth about Robin from you for so long. In a way, I feel equally responsible for her actions.'

'I think you are being rather harsh on yourself. It is one thing to own up to one's own responsibilities in life, quite another to shoulder someone else's, no matter how close you feel to them. Robin did what she wanted to do.'

'I just wish, I could have stopped her.'

'She followed her own path as she saw fit. There is nothing you or anyone else could have done.'

'Still I look back and try to think if I could have done anything differently, to make her feel more secure and loved, once I came to know that Helen was Robin.'

'I meant to ask you about that. When did you first recognise her?'

'I didn't. Strangely, it was she who recognised me the instant she saw me. We met at the dinner that Sofia gave in her honour, when Helen first came to stay at Falcon's Crest.'

'Yes, I remember that evening.'

'It was on the same evening, right after dinner, that Helen came up to me and asked me outright if I was her brother 'Dusty.' You could have knocked me down with a feather. I was overjoyed to find her again. You see, I thought I had lost her forever. We went for a walk afterwards and she told me about her life after her adoption by the Cavendishes. And I told her how my life had panned out including my meeting and consequent marriage with Pamela and the birth of our daughter Anne. I requested her to keep quiet about our origins and relationship for obvious reasons. I didn't want you to know my real identity.'

Judge Wilson asked, 'But why, John. Why didn't you trust me?'

John hung his head and then finally said with some difficulty, 'You see, as children both Robin and I had hated you with a passion. We believed that you had destroyed our happy family and that you were directly responsible for our parents' deaths. I assumed that you would fling me out by my ear if you ever came to know that I was my mother's son.'

'I can't blame you. I'm glad we are having this little talk. It may help clear some of the confusion in our lives. I'd like to come clean and tell you what really happened all those years ago between your mother and me. I won't deny that I was very fond of your mother. Over a period of six months, we worked in close quarters and fell in love with each other. I'm sorry but that is the truth. It all happened so quickly. She was like a breath of fresh air in my otherwise dull and dreary life. For both our sakes, and to avoid any further pain, I'll not go into details of who led who on, and so forth. Suffice to say that we were both consenting adults who had, for the first time in our lives, found a passionate love with one another. And then I made a huge mistake that I regret to this day. I offered to set her up as my mistress. Although I still think that I would not have had the courage, to do such a thing, if I had not felt that she was open to my suggestion. I couldn't have been more wrong!

To cut a long story short, she was livid. She had expected me to offer her marriage but I couldn't – we were both married with children. She suggested that we each get a divorce but I told her that it would ruin my career and I had my children to think of. I told her that the only option left to us, was for me to set her up in a comfortable place close by so that we could continue to meet without hindrance. She turned me down flatly and told me to go to the blazes. We had a huge row and she left me.

I don't know what happened that evening, after she got home but the next thing I knew was that your father came to my doorstep and started shooting at me. You know the rest. As for Bedlow's covert allegations that I hired someone to kill her, don't think that the officers back in those days, were such fools. As bad luck would have it, one of the eye witnesses had indeed been in my employ years ago, but luckily he had no contact with me for years. They investigated me, grilled both him and me and let me off the hook only after they were convinced I had no role to play in the railway accident.'

John spoke, 'Thank you. I think I needed to hear that but there is one more thing I'd like to know.'

'What is it?'

'Well, Dad, the newspapers have been going on about my father's case being assigned to Judge Greene and his consequent sentencing to Dartmoor. Did you have a role in that?'

'I have to admit, that there, I was guilty. I did use my authority to pull a few strings to make that happen. Not my proudest moment but I didn't want the man to come out in a few years and finish the job he had started. I convinced myself at the time, that I did it out of a motive of self defence. I am sorry, John.'

'I am sorry too. But I suppose, if I were in your shoes, I'd have probably done the same thing.'

'I very much doubt it, John. You are a good man and in all your actions, over the years, have shown me that no matter what happens, ultimately the choice lies with each one of us, to do the right thing. I don't know if I can ever make it up to you, but I do want to do the right thing by you now.'

'You already have, dad. More than you know.'

Chapter
Twenty Seven

Rachel came out of anaesthesia after her surgery at the Cottage Hospital. They had successfully removed the bullet from her arm. Sofia was by her side when she came to.

She was still groggy but she managed to squeak, 'Jeremy, where is Jeremy?'

'I'll get him for you, honey. He just stepped out. Both the Chief Inspector and Judge Wilson wanted a word with him.'

By the time Sofia came in accompanied by Jeremy, Rachel was asleep again.

This time he stayed by her side.

When she awoke an hour later, she found him asleep in an armchair pulled up close beside her bed. He was holding her hand. She tugged his hand and he woke with a start.

'How are you feeling, darling?'

'Awful. It's like my mouth is full of cotton wool. And my arm hurts.'

'It stopped a bullet, darling. The least it can do is hurt a bit. My brave girl, you'll be fine. Luckily, it was just a flesh wound.'

'Luckily, I'm not dead,' Rachel grumbled.

'Luck has nothing to do with it. Helen was a terrible shot. How she missed at a distance of two feet is downright puzzling. If she had shot all her victims, instead of poisoning or drowning them, I reckon they'd all still be alive!' Jeremy joked, trying to cheer her up.

'Have I ever told that you that I'm glad you're a detective. Because, with your bedside manner, you'd have made the world's worst doctor in the history of medical science.'

'And she's back! My darling!'

II

Four days later, they were all gathered at Ravenrock House. Chief Inspector Harrow had requested the Judge to hold a gathering of 'all souls' involved in the case. While Helen's confession in front of five witnesses had tied up several loose ends, there was one point on which the police still needed clarity. The Judge had invited everyone associated with the case. Apart from Chief Inspector Harrow and the residents of Ravenrock House – Antonio, John and Timothy, among those present were - Sofia and Henry Cavendish, Jeremy and Rachel, Dr. Meadows, both the police inspectors – Thomas and Parker and last but not least - Constable Goole. PC Goole's job was to take copious notes through the session that would later be included in the case file.

Rachel's arm was still in a sling. She had been discharged from the hospital a few hours ago. Dr. Meadows had just changed the dressing on the wound and was happy to note that the stitches were healing nicely. Timothy and Antonio had brought in some extra chairs. Everyone had settled down in the Judge's study.

Chief Inspector Harrow was the first to speak. 'I thank you all for being here on such short notice but I have to return to London by the morning train and I wanted your help in closing the case.'

There were murmurs of 'that's alright' and 'don't mention it' around the room.

'We know that Helen Cavendish or Robin Jones, as we now know her, killed several people in an act of vengeance against Judge Wilson's family. Psychological profiling tells us that her aim was not to kill Judge Wilson directly, but to inflict the same pain of familial loss on Judge Wilson that she and her brother had undergone as children. So one by one, she systematically went about eliminating the Judge's family and if she had not been caught when she was, she would have continued with her plan and more lives would have been lost. This was a complicated case and we have statements from all of you that give us a clear idea as to the modus operandi of the crimes committed, but there is one point on which we need further clarification, Ms. Markham, how did you know she was the killer? And when did you first begin to suspect that your friend was behind the crimes?'

Rachel spoke, 'In retrospect, there were quite a few things that tipped me off. I think the first time I got a hint that something was amiss, was when I saw how emotionally strung she was over Captain John Griffin's car accident. You see, the intended victim had always been Antonio or Evelyn. She was riddled with guilt that she had almost killed her own brother. At the time, I misread her concern to be romantic love but it was far deeper than that; it was the love of a little sister towards an adored older brother.'

Sofia was still puzzled. 'Yes, I remember, we spoke about it one evening. But Rachel, that can't be it. What convinced you that *she* was Robin?'

'I think it was the report from the Swiss Clinic in the library that set me thinking. It opened my eyes to the possibility that Helen could be adopted. From there to the conclusion that Robin could have been a name for a girl and that she was Robin, was just a matter of time. There were a few other things along the way that impressed upon me that she could be the killer. The way she described losing her mother... she told me, *that she was trying to make peace with all that was snatched away from her.* Her dark twisted paintings. I found one, where she had twisted the paint into menacing clouds around a woman's head. I later identified the woman in the painting as Edith from a picture on this shelf. She was definitely an artist at heart because everything she felt, even the darkness in her soul, came through her paint brush on to the canvas.'

John said, 'My poor little Robin. She had great talent and life gave her a second chance at a bright future but sadly, she chose to cling to the demons of the past. I wish it had been otherwise. Strangely enough, just a few days ago she had given me a lecture on the benefits of letting go of the past.' He gave them a sad smile. 'I wish, she had done it herself. I've lost her for good now. But I can't help thinking that she has left me with a valuable lesson in forgiveness. And I do hope that despite everything, when you all remember her, it will be with a sense of forgiveness and mercy.'

Judge Wilson said, 'You are right. I speak from experience when I say that sometimes, certain events in life overpower our sense of right and wrong and we feel powerless in their wake. It is not hard to understand, why Robin did what she did. I also know that neither Lucy nor I ever dreamt that our meeting would end in such disastrous consequences for all concerned. One lives and learns. However, John is right. Forgiveness is the only possible answer. And I can only hope that all those concerned, can also forgive my role in these events.'

Rachel said with kindness, 'You both are right. She was a dear friend, Marcus but a lost soul. You are not alone in wishing that things could have worked out differently. I too, feel that had I handled her confrontation differently she might still be alive. But, as things go, I think it's important to remember that it is now in the past and we cannot go back and change anything. I, for one, will always remember her with love. And the good times that we shared.'

Inspector Thomas concluded, 'I think, Chief Inspector, we can safely assume that this case is now, closed.'

The Chief Inspector stood up and said, 'Quite. Thank you all for your time. And now, we must be on our way.'

As Jeremy and Rachel accompanied the police officers to the door, Chief Inspector Harrow addressed Rachel, 'This has been a most informative evening. Ms Markham. This is the second case that you have helped us solve. I think, like your husband, you ought to consider a professional career in law enforcement. You would be quite a force to reckon with.'

Rachel said, 'Chief Inspector, that is very kind of you, but after almost being killed, twice in a span of one year, I think I must decline your kind offer.'

The Chief Inspector smiled as he shook hands with both of them and took his leave. Jeremy turned to Rachel and said, 'Thank goodness for small mercies. But somehow, darling, I don't know why, but I get the distinct feeling that your declaration brings a certain phrase to mind. Could it be, "famous last words"?'

Epilogue

Three months later...

Sofia helped Henry Cavendish to come to terms with losing his beloved daughter, by involving him completely in designing a new nursery wing for the impending arrival. Henry had wanted to ship Oswald in, once again from New York, and it took all of Sofia's tact and diplomacy to dissuade him from doing so and convince him that they could design the space, by themselves. They were united in their grief over Helen's loss, however, the hectic activity of building and decorating the new wing in the house kept them both from brooding over the past events that had stirred the nation's interest. Interestingly, the wing was being built as an extension to the ground floor of the house, and extended to the space where the garden shed once stood. The nursery would open out to the flower garden.

Judge Wilson set up a comfortable trust fund for John Griffin, who used a major part of it, to start building an orphanage, which he decided to name, 'Robin's Nest'. He had already used Jeremy and Chief Inspector Harrow's help to get in touch with prison authorities. Robin's Nest would cater not only to orphans but also be a home to children who were not technically orphaned, but left bereft when either or both parents were incarcerated to long prison terms. On a suggestion from Jeremy, John approached Tom Bedlow for help in running the orphanage. Bedlow agreed with alacrity and to everyone's surprise, he roped Marge Harding into the project as well. To their further surprise, she enthusiastically agreed to handle the complete administration of the orphanage. She was up for retirement from the Yard in two years, coincidentally, the same amount of time, it would take for the orphanage to be up and running.

Antonio went back to racing cars with renewed vigour, with a good deal of encouragement from Judge Wilson. He was now in Bari, Italy, preparing to take the Bari Grand Prix by storm. Inspired by him, Timothy too began preparing in earnest, for the Dartmouth Royal Regatta to be held in August. With architects and engineers visiting with plans for the upcoming orphanage, Ravenrock had now become a hub of useful activity.

Jeremy and Rachel decided to spend a week in London and were greeted warmly by Duke Wellington, as soon as they stepped off the train at Waterloo station. As they drove out from the station, he regaled them with a humorous rendition of his Scottish adventure and his new found love for the charming ladies – both young and old Anna, whom he had met. He also informed them that he was saving up to visit them again next summer.

As promised, Jeremy took Rachel on a visit to Scotland Yard where she finally met Marge Harding. It did not surprise Jeremy that both ladies got along like a house on fire. As Jeremy went upstairs to meet the Chief Inspector, Marge took Rachel for a tour of Scotland Yard and finally showed her the archives. While walking about they spoke of unsolved cases.

Marge told her about a very interesting case, in the recent past that was yet to be solved. It involved a certain retired Colonel Riverton, whose family had been in India for the past three generations. Apparently, the Colonel himself had been associated with an Indian Maharajah of a small princely state, in his capacity as an administrator and trainer for the Maharajah's Polo team. The trouble was, while the murder had taken place during the polo season in India, two years ago, some of the people who had been suspects at the time, had since returned to England, and the murderer had never been caught. Colonel Riverton, himself, was now in London, on behalf of the Maharajah, who wanted to get to the bottom of this case, once and for all. Rachel listened with awestruck wonder as visions of marble palaces, polo matches and colonial life floated in front of her eyes. Just then, Jeremy joined them after his meeting with Chief Inspector Harrow. As they said their goodbyes, thanked Marge Harding and walked out of Scotland Yard, he told Rachel that he had something interesting to discuss.

'Darling, Chief Inspector Harrow just introduced me to an old friend of his, Colonel Riverton - a most interesting chap. He's asked us to dinner at The Savoy. It seems, that after hearing glowing reports from Harrow about our, rather 'your' detecting abilities, he may have a commission for us that could include an all expenses paid trip to India. I did tell him that you were done with your 'life of crime' but I wondered if you would be interested in at least having dinner with the man.'

'I wouldn't miss it for the world! Oh, Jeremy, how delightful. I'd love a trip to India,' she said, her eyes shining brightly.

'How about we just go for dinner first, eh?' Jeremy said with a laugh.

Rachel retorted, 'Jeremy Richards, it's time to put on your solar topi. We are going to India, whether you like it or not!'

'I know, I already said yes to him,' he said with a mischievous smile, as Rachel's eyes lit up with unspoken promises of travel to an exotic faraway land and the challenge of yet another mystery to explore.

$15,95
5/15

T 577875

DUE

JUN 2 4 2015
SEP 3 0 2015
OCT 1 0 2015

NOV 1 0 2017

PRINTED IN U.S.A.

41498150R00138

Made in the USA
Lexington, KY
17 May 2015